### "I've wanted you since I saw you lying in a puddle of water in the parking lot," Ian murmured.

Piper laughed softly, then pushed gently at his chest. "Speaking of puddles...my cake!" She stepped away from him and walked toward the refrigerator. "Do you want whipped cream?" At his nod, she added, "Cherries, too?"

"Sure," he said, swallowing. The woman was killing him. "Why not?"

She carried the cake to the table. "Well, dig in."

Although he'd been craving something sweeter, Ian took a mouthful, then nodded appreciatively. "It's great. Have a bite." He held a spoonful to her lips, managing to drizzle sauce on her chin. She moved to wipe it away, but he stopped her hand. "Let me." He leaned forward and licked the sauce from her chin, nipping along her jaw. Reaching past her, he dipped his finger in the chocolate, then stroked it down the side of her neck. "Oh, look," he murmured, proceeding to lick it off, inch by delectable inch.

The dessert abandoned, he stood and pulled her closer to him, burying his face in her cleavage. She moaned, swaying into him, and his body leaped in response. "Piper," he whispered against her skin, "I *need* to make love to you."

# Stephanie
# BOND

## Manhunting
### in Mississippi

**BONUS: An original story by JULIE KENNER**

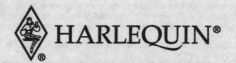

# HARLEQUIN®

TORONTO • NEW YORK • LONDON
AMSTERDAM • PARIS • SYDNEY • HAMBURG
STOCKHOLM • ATHENS • TOKYO • MILAN • MADRID
PRAGUE • WARSAW • BUDAPEST • AUCKLAND

ISBN 0-373-83553-1

MANHUNTING IN MISSISSIPPI

Copyright © 2003 by Harlequin Books S.A.

The publisher acknowledges the copyright holders of the individual works as follows:

MANHUNTING IN MISSISSIPPI
Copyright © 1998 by Stephanie Hauck

WRAPPED AND READY
Copyright © 2001 by Harlequin Books S.A.

Visit us at www.eHarlequin.com

Printed In U.S.A.

# CONTENTS

## Books by Stephanie Bond

# MANHUNTING IN MISSISSIPPI

## Stephanie Bond

This book is dedicated to Brenda Chin,
my adventurous editor,
who trusts me to run with my stories.

# CHAPTER ONE

*ALWAYS A BRIDESMAID*...and always broke. Fighting the phone cord, Piper Shepherd glanced in the mirror at the yellow satin dress she held draped over her torso. With her cropped, dark hair, the ruffled netting around the shoulders made her look like a molting bird in a nest, but it would do. "Personally, Justine, I think lemon yellow would be stunning for an August wedding."

Her friend sighed at the other end of the phone, obviously unconvinced. "Mother says yellow won't stand out in the outdoor photos. Besides, didn't Barb have yellow for her bridesmaids' dresses?"

Piper winced. "Did she?" She tossed the dress on her bed, then withdrew a long, off-the-shoulder lavender gown from the closet and held it under her chin. A sloshed usher had ripped off a ribbon rosette during someone's reception, but the dress was serviceable. "How about lilac?"

"Hmm," Justine mused, tapping her fingernail

against the phone. "Nah, I don't think it would complement Stewart's carrottop. Besides, didn't Sarah use lilac?"

Piper frowned. "Did she?" She tossed the dress on top of the other one and withdrew an emerald organza mini with a sequined cape. "Green would look great next to Stew's red hair—maybe something short and snazzy to catch the sunlight?"

"I don't think so," Justine said slowly. "Green makes me look sallow. Besides, didn't Joann use green?"

A low throbbing started in Piper's temple. "Did she?" She discarded the dress, then pivoted back to her closet and flipped through the hangers. "Mauve?"

"Carol."

"Fuchsia?"

"Cindy."

"Sapphire?"

"Hmm, wasn't that your mom's color?"

Piper grunted. "For which wedding?"

"To Roger, I think."

Biting back a disrespectful remark, Piper forced her fingers to travel on. "Ruby? Teal? Metallic gold?"

"Jan, Tina and Jennifer."

Piper jammed her hand through her short hair.

"My God, Justine, how on earth do you remember who used which color in what wedding?"

"I just do," Justine said, and Piper could picture her friend's thin shoulders shrugging. "But then I've always loved weddings—unlike you, Piper. If you'd spent less time moaning about the high heels and more time checking out the groomsmen, you'd be getting married, too. Out of twenty-three of us, you're the last one, you know."

Piper frowned. "Not true—Tillie is still single." Not that being in the same company as their chubby, hypochondriac sorority sister was anything to boast about.

"Uh-uh, she got engaged three weeks ago—haven't you heard?"

Piper yanked down the phone cord, unaware she had managed to wind it around her neck. "Who to?" she croaked, then unwound herself with an impatient twist.

"She spent so much time at the clinic, she managed to snare a doctor—her diamond is a freaking boulder."

For an instant, Piper experienced a pang of panic. Even allergic, insomniac, headachy, PMS-ing Tillie had snagged a man—and a rich one, to boot. She sighed and glanced at her watch. She'd promised her grandmother she'd be over to help box up some things for her upcoming move.

"Piper, are you there, or is your life passing before your eyes?"

"I'm here," she snapped. "And thirty-one doesn't exactly make me eligible for a discount at the bingo parlor."

Justine sighed dramatically. "People are beginning to talk, Piper. You would tell me, wouldn't you, if you were, um…you know."

"I don't know what the heck you're talking about."

"You know—gay."

Piper dropped the phone, then chased it across the floor as the spiral cord contracted to pull it home. "No, I'm not gay!" she yelled as she dived on the handset, juggled it and finally wrestled it to her ear. "How could you even *think* such a thing?" she barked into the phone.

Her friend tapped her fingers against the receiver again. "Piper, I can't remember you ever having a lasting relationship with a man. A few dates, yeah, but were you ever serious about anyone?"

Piper pursed her lips and fidgeted with the cord. "I guess I'm picky."

"I'm telling you, Piper, you'd better start hunting for a man before all the good ones are gone."

"Justine, you're two hundred miles away in Tupelo where the men are plentiful *and* passable. I'm in Mudville—when you visited, did you happen to see anyone who would put me in the manhunting mood?"

"You've got a point." Her friend hummed in sympathy. "You really should move to the city—any city."

"Except Blythe Industries can't find cheap labor to run their plant in the city."

Justine scoffed. "Oh, and no other company in all of Mississippi could use a food scientist?"

Piper pursed her lips. "Maybe—but then I'd be farther away from Gran, and you've got to admit, I have a terrific job."

"True—most women wouldn't *have* to be paid to design desserts."

"Well, it's not all fudge sauce and whipped cream, Justine. It's harder than it sounds."

"Yeah, yeah…bottom line, Piper, you can't let your career or your family get in the way of finding your soulmate, your dream man—your hero."

"The only hero I've seen in Mudville, Mississippi, is the sandwich special at Limbo's Deli."

"Oh, come on. There has to be at least one eligible man in that podunk town. You're going to have to extend yourself a little, you know. See and be seen.''

''I'm not so sure I want to see and be seen at a tractor pull.''

''You're going to have to work for this one, Piper. You need a man plan.''

Piper laughed. ''Which comes first—the man or the plan?''

''Do you have a good-looking co-worker? Boss?''

Her assistant, Rich, was good-looking. But it was a well-guarded secret that he was gay, too. And her boss, Edmund, was a married man, besides being old enough to be her father. ''No one remotely eligible.''

''Neighbor?''

''Nada.''

''UPS man?''

''He's a woman.''

''Well, you've got three whole months to come up with a dance partner for the wedding—all the men in the wedding party are taken.''

Piper flopped down on top of the dress pile, sending the hangers clanging. ''Oh, well, that should be a cinch. After all, ballroom dancing is *such* a popular pastime in Mudville.''

''You'll think of something. Cheer up—I'll bet

every happily married woman had a strategy to snag their man. Take Stew, for example. He dragged his feet for three years. Then, when I told him I had a job offer in Tennessee, he fell to his knees.''

Piper frowned. Her bedroom ceiling needed to be painted. ''I didn't know you had a job offer in Tennessee.''

''I didn't.''

''Oh.''

''Piper, it's *our* job to convince men they can't live without us. Keep your eyes open for someone older—maybe a divorced man.''

''I'm not so sure I want a retread.''

Justine clucked. ''Sophie says men are better husbands the second time around—you don't have nearly as much training to do.''

''This is starting to sound like a lot of work.''

Justine sighed noisily. ''Piper, do you want to grow old alone?''

Shutting her eyes against the welling misery, Piper relented, puffing her heated cheeks. ''No.''

''Then you'd better start doing something about it.''

''Okay, okay, I get the message. Can we please change the subject?''

''Aha!'' Justine whooped. ''I just thought of the

perfect color for my bridesmaids' dresses—
salmon!''

Piper bit back a groan, bounced up from the bed
and walked her fingers over the collection of gowns
still hanging in the cramped wardrobe. Burgundy,
tangerine, moss green, silver, baby blue, pink, coral,
eggplant, peach and plum.

But no salmon.

IAN BENTLEY BLINKED at the thick gold band,
topped with two rows of sparkling diamonds, then
glanced across the table to Meredith. "M-marry
you?"

"Sure." She shrugged her lovely shoulders, a
dry smile curving her glazed red lips. "I won a trip
to Europe for top sales, but I'm only allowed to
have a spouse go with me—no 'significant others.'''

Ian pursed his lips and studied her classically
beautiful face and mane of blond hair, which no
doubt contributed to her sales success. Meredith
was a walking billboard for the line of cosmetics
she sold to department stores, more striking than
most of the supermodels who endorsed the prod-
ucts. But was hers a face he could wake up to for
the rest of his life? "Meredith, forgive me, but a

trip doesn't seem like a great reason to get married.''

She laughed and waved off his concern. ''Silly, I know that, but the trip started me thinking. Why the hell not get married? We spend most nights together anyway—*when* we're both in town,'' she added. ''Getting married is the next logical step.'' She leaned forward and touched his hand. ''Come on, Ian, neither one of us is getting any younger.''

The uneasiness that gurgled in Ian's empty stomach ballooned into dread, then full-fledged terror. In the space of a few seconds, the innocent, quick lunch had morphed into a life-altering experience. Meredith was an elegant woman, an immaculate dresser and a skilled lover. He enjoyed her company very much. But did he love her?

Ian skewered the elusive concept and turned it over in his mind like a rotisserie. Would he even recognize the emotion if it sneaked up on him? He always thought he'd be married, perhaps even have a child or two, before the age of forty. But forty was approaching more quickly than he'd expected, and he was still waiting for someone to capture his heart the way his mother had captured his father's nearly five decades ago.

Meredith's flawless face lost some of its sparkle.

"Gee, Ian, you look like you siphoned gas and swallowed a mouthful."

Straightening in his suddenly uncomfortable chair, he squeezed the gray ring box and grappled for the right words. "You caught me a little off guard, Meredith."

She angled her blond head at him. "That would be the idea behind a surprise, wouldn't it?"

A weak laugh erupted from his tight throat as moisture broke out along his hairline.

"Try it on," she urged, lifting her wineglass for a sip, then added, "your left hand."

His gaze dropped back to the ring. Ian extracted it carefully, marveling how an expensive bauble could come attached with so much emotional baggage. "It's very nice," he murmured, estimating that two carats' worth of diamonds studded the gold band. Meredith's taste ran a bit on the flashy side. With his heart pounding, he slid the ring onto his third finger, then gave her a tight smile. "Perfect fit." *Dammit.*

"You don't have to answer right away," she offered, withdrawing a black-cased lipstick and mirror for a quick touch-up. "Wear the ring for a few days, see how you like the idea of being a married man. If you say yes, we'll simply buy me a band to match."

"I'm leaving tomorrow on business," he blurted, changing the subject awkwardly, but suddenly anticipating the trip he'd been dreading only moments ago.

Meredith's eyes lit up. "Anywhere interesting?"

Although she occasionally accompanied him from Chicago to Los Angeles or New York, Ian felt nearly giddy with relief that she wouldn't be so eager to join him on this trip. He forced disappointment into his voice. "Afraid not—Mudville, Mississippi, population twelve hundred."

Her slender nose wrinkled. "What's in Mudville, Mississippi?"

"The plant that packages desserts for my Italian diners."

"Oooh, the butterscotch cheesecake?"

He smiled and nodded. "Among others."

Wincing, she patted her flat tummy with a manicured hand. "That settles it—with bathing-suit season around the corner, I definitely can't go."

Ian made a clicking sound with his cheek and tried to look disappointed. "Maybe next time."

"Why are you going?"

"I'm planning to franchise the coffeehouses next year, and I think a designer dessert would improve their marketability—you know, something catchy."

She narrowed her almond-shaped eyes. "I meant,

why are *you* going? Don't you have someone to take care of that kind of thing?''

"Well…yes," he admitted, not without a certain amount of guilt. His vice president of marketing had made the same point just last week when Ian had returned from a plant in Illinois. And his doctor had warned him only yesterday to delegate more work at the office. Frustration pushed at his chest, causing him to respond more vehemently than the situation warranted. "But I think the importance of this project justifies a firsthand consultation with the company's food scientists."

Meredith's eyes widened slightly, then she inclined her head. "When it comes to food, you seem to know what the public wants." One eyebrow arched and she smirked. "How are the kiddie parlors selling?"

Glad for the change in subject, he smiled wide. "Great so far. Pizza and trampolines seem to be a profitable mix."

"Go figure," she said, her dry tone a clear indication of how she felt about having kids, hearing kids or just plain *seeing* kids—a fact which needled him slightly. She blotted her lipstick with her folded napkin. "How long will you be in…Mudville, is it?"

"Oh, I don't know…as long as it takes to get a

good prototype. Maybe a week, maybe more. Sometimes these small-town plants are not as prepared as they should be for presentations.''

Her frown quickly turned into a sweet smile as she reached forward to pat his left hand. ''Well, at least I won't have to worry about you finding someone else in a place called Mudville. If it's as desolate and godforsaken as it sounds, you'll have lots of peace and quiet to consider my proposal.''

Ian conjured up a smile and hoped it wasn't as shaky as his knees. At this moment, Mudville seemed like a haven, a slow little one-horse town where he could *forget* about the proposal for a few days. Fresh air, good-tasting water, maybe even a fishing trip or two…and no women bent on dragging him to the altar.

''HI, GRAN.'' Piper dropped a kiss on her grandmother's silky cheek. ''Sorry I'm late. Justine is obsessing over her wedding plans.''

Dressed in gray sweats, Ellen Falkner radiated youth—seventy-five going on forty-five, she was much too young-looking for the title of ''granny,'' a name she insisted on nonetheless.

Granny Falkner smiled wide, tucked a strand of convincing light brown hair beneath her blue bandanna, then planted her hands on her hips. ''Don't fret, Piper. There's still plenty to do.'' She frowned and glanced around the living room, shaking her head. ''How does one accumulate so much junk?''

At least two dozen brown boxes lined the perimeter of the weathered room, stacked atop jumbled furniture. The cabbage-rose wallpaper Piper had always loved suddenly appeared yellowed and dated next to the bright squares where pictures had once hung. Stripped of its window dressings, the tall-ceilinged parlor looked half-naked and lonely, as if already pining for its mistress.

''Gran,'' Piper said softly, ''after forty years, you're allowed to have accumulated a few knick-knacks.''

''I know,'' her grandmother said, caressing the wooden mantel. ''And I'm really going to miss this old house.'' Then she turned a bright smile toward Piper. ''But six years alone is plenty long enough. I hate to leave the house empty, but Nate would want me to move on, and Greenbay Ridge looks like my kind of place.'' She winked. ''I can learn to line dance and still be close to you.''

''You'll be the social butterfly of the entire retirement community, Gran. And the real-estate agent will find a buyer soon.''

Her grandmother's forehead wrinkled. ''I wish you would take the house, Piper.''

Piper shrugged, guilt riding through her. "I told you I'd be glad to move in with you. It would add only five minutes to my commute."

"Which would be wonderful for me, but not for you, dear. No, we both need to get on with our lives, but I was hoping you'd be looking for a home when I was ready to move."

Yearning bubbled within Piper, but she struggled to maintain a calm expression. Despite its dubious location in the outskirts of Mudville, she *did* want the big old house she so dearly loved, and for years she'd been putting aside every spare dime hoping she'd be able to buy it someday. Her finances still fell short of the mark, but if she received the bonus she was hoping for, she'd be within striking distance. But in case things didn't work out, she had sworn the real-estate agent to secrecy. Piper chose her words carefully. "Gran, I can't afford to buy this place, and I'm certainly not going to let you give it to me."

Her grandmother shook her head and frowned. "I know Mudville isn't the most exciting place to spend the rest of your life, but I did so want you and your children to have this home."

"Gran," Piper chided, "be practical. You have to have money to live on." Then she grinned. "And in case you hadn't noticed, I'm not pregnant."

She was rewarded with a wry, wrinkled smile. "Not unless it was an immaculate conception, I'd wager."

"Gran!"

Granny Falkner angled her head. "Really, dear, you conduct yourself like a nun."

Shock thickened her tongue. "I...I don't want to talk about my, um—"

"Chastity?"

"Well, I'm not exactly a vir—" Piper stopped and swallowed. "A Virgo." She laughed weakly and jammed her hands on her hips in a desperate attempt to look innocent. "I mean, I'm not exactly a Virgo," she repeated in a squeaky voice. "B-because I'm a Pisces...as you know, Gran." She cleared her throat noisily and scrutinized the toes of her leather clogs.

Granny Falkner laughed. "You young people think you invented sex. Well, I'm here to tell you, your grandfather and I could have filed for a patent or two of our own."

Piper blinked and held up her hands. "Gran, I really don't want to hear this."

"Relax, Piper, I'm not going to embarrass you. I'm simply trying to get you to open up." She reached out and ran her thumb over Piper's cheek.

"You still don't realize how lovely you are—with that face, you could have any man you wanted."

"Spoken like a true grandmother."

Sharp blue eyes, which she'd inherited, stared back at her. "Did someone break your heart, dear? Some young man in college?"

The concern in her gran's face sent a swell of love through Piper's chest. The older woman knew all too well the grief Piper had suffered all her life. Her mother didn't even know the name of the man who had fathered her. How could she tell her grandmother that she'd lived in fear of repeating her mother's mistakes? That she'd been embarrassed to even introduce her outrageously flirtatious mother to the young men she dated? That she'd purposely ignored boys to whom she was attracted so she wouldn't have to deal with the overpowering sexual rush that made people do crazy things with their lives?

Her few intimate encounters had been with timid, fumbling boys who'd been even more inept than she'd imagined herself to be. She managed a comforting smile. "I met and dated some nice guys in college, but my heart is perfectly intact."

"And is there a current beau I don't know about?"

Piper pursed her lips, then replied in a singsongy voice. "Noooooo."

Her grandmother sighed and crossed her arms. "I know you're independent, dear, but sharing your life with the right person can be an extraordinary experience."

A pang of longing pierced Piper, but she decided to make light of the comment. Her grandmother worried enough without Piper fueling the maternal fire. "Gran, I have other priorities right now, like establishing my professional reputation, paying off school loans, maybe even building a nest egg for myself."

"Is your job still going well?" She handed Piper a red bandanna for her hair.

Piper immediately recognized the worn cloth as the handkerchief her grandfather had carried in the back pocket of his pants. She covered her hair and stretched her arms to tie the ends at the nape of her neck. "My job's fine. I'm starting a new project this week to persuade our biggest client to extend their contract. Wish me luck!" *If her grandmother only knew how much was riding on the creation of one little dessert.*

"Good luck, dear. But all work and no play…" Innuendo colored the older woman's voice as it trailed off.

A sly grin broke out on Piper's face. "Gran, I'm letting my sorority sisters weed out the eager, needy men."

Her grandmother laughed, then wagged a finger. "Just don't wait *too* long."

Piper narrowed her eyes. "Have you been talking to Justine, because this is starting to sound like a conspiracy."

Gran's laugh echoed in the empty room and she raised her arms in defeat. "Okay, I'll stop so we can get some work done."

Piper looked around the room, struck once again by the unfamiliar emptiness. She'd spent endless summers in this house, and as many weekends and holidays as possible, since her mother hadn't exactly been a nurturing caregiver. Panic stirred in her stomach at the sight of the furniture she'd played on as a child pushed against the walls, queued up haphazardly as if awaiting deportation. Beneath the window stood the wooden coffee table. Her initials, which she'd carved with her grandfather's Swiss army knife when she was seven, were still on the leg. And next to it, the armless padded rocking chair Gran had sat in when she sewed while Piper sprawled on the floor, stringing buttons with a dulled needle. She swallowed. "Where do I start, Gran?"

"I'm taking the couch, love seat, end tables and lamps, plus the bedroom suite and the kitchen table and chairs." Her grandmother shrugged and grinned. "Everything else is yours."

Mouth open, Piper turned. "Mine? But Gran, I don't have space for all this." *Unless I buy this house.*

Undaunted, Granny Falkner continued, "You can leave it here until the house sells, then put the whole kit and caboodle in storage."

Piper took a deep breath and nodded obediently. "Okay, I'll think of something."

"Those boxes are personal things I gathered for you—let's load them into your van so we'll have more room to move around in here."

Staggering under the weight of the first box, Piper laughed. "What *is* all this stuff?"

Granny Falkner waved her hand in the air, then picked up another carton that appeared just as heavy. "Just books and such, a lot of old nonsense I saved for far too long. Go through it and keep what strikes your fancy and throw away the rest."

Piper walked back through the kitchen and held open the screen door with her elbow. "Mom called last night. She said to say hello."

"Why didn't she call and tell me herself?" her grandmother asked airily.

Sighing, Piper said, "I suggested the same thing."

"She's mad because I said something about that lazy bum she's shacking up with."

"She says they're going to get married."

Granny Falkner's laugh crackled dryly. "After four trips to the altar, you'd think her judgment would improve."

Nodding in mute agreement, Piper tingled with shame. Despite her grandmother's wish to see her settled down, she wondered what Gran would think of the manhunt on which she had decided to embark. Probably not much, she decided with a sideways glance at the woman whose wisdom and advice she treasured.

Her grandmother lowered her box onto the floor of the van. "In fifty-five years, the only thing Maggie managed to do right is have you. And how you turned out so well, I'll never know." She put her arm around Piper's shoulders as they walked back to the house. "I live in eternal hope that your mother will be just like you when she grows up."

Her grandmother's words reverberated in Piper's head during the next few hours of packing and dusting and cleaning. Her mother's track record was frightening—would her own burgeoning desire for male companionship color her judgment, too?

Wouldn't she be better off without a man than launching into a series of roller-coaster relationships? She didn't know the first thing about finding a husband—her mother certainly wasn't much of an example, and at the time, she hadn't cared enough to study her sorority sisters in action. Worse, by deciding to buy her grandmother's house and stay in Mudville, she'd narrowed the field of eligible men tremendously. Piper sighed. In the unlikely event that she did find a suitable dating prospect in town, she'd just have to wing it.

But on the late drive back to her town house, peering out the window at the forlorn little town she had made home a year ago, Piper had serious doubts about finding her dream man in the immediate vicinity. A decidedly garish neon sign read Welcome to Mudville. To make matters worse, the four center letters had expired, reducing the town greeting to Welcome to Mule.

The trip down Main Street took her past three used car lots festooned in multicolored plastic flags, nine beauty shops, six video-rental stores, two tanning parlors, ''And a partridge in a pear tree,'' she murmured as she pulled to a stop at one of the town's two stoplights. Mudville consisted of two square blocks of dilapidated buildings and a few side streets, plus one fast-food restaurant where the town's teenagers and desperate adults hung out. Then she chastised herself. *People in glass houses...*

The blare of a horn caused her to jerk her head toward the vehicle on her right. Too late, she recognized the smoke-belching, rattletrap sports car of Lenny Kern, her neighbor's son, who seemed determined to live at home until he could pool his social security check with his mother's. With a thick paw, he motioned for her to roll down her window, and after a reluctant sigh, she obliged.

"Hey, Piper, what's shakin'?" he bawled above the glass-shattering decibels of Hank Williams, Sr.

"Hey, Lenny," she said with a tight smile.

"Wanna go for a ride?" he asked, grinning wide.

"No, thanks."

"Aw, come on, Piper, *Top Gun* is playing at the dollar theater."

She grimaced. "I rented it several years ago."

"Oh, really?" He frowned, and bit his lower lip.

Thankfully, the light turned green. "So long, Lenny," she said, pulling away from the intersection. Her neighbor had been trying to wear her down into going out with him since she moved in. And she wasn't *that* lonely...yet.

When she arrived at her town house, Piper parked, took out one of the boxes her grandmother

had given her and went inside. She sprawled on the
living-room floor in front of the television. With the
remote, she tuned into a rerun of a comedy that
hadn't been funny the first time, then pulled the box
toward her and placed it between her spread legs,
curiosity coursing through her.

The smell of mothballs, dried paper and stale
flowers filled her nostrils as she lifted the lid. The
box held a hodgepodge of memorabilia: dusty
photo albums, yellowed songbooks, thick seventy-
eight-size phonograph records and curling post-
cards. She thumbed through old issues of *Look*
magazine, and smiled at hokey rhymes on ancient
greeting cards. There were several paper-thin em-
broidered handkerchiefs, an invitation to her grandmother's high-school graduation and a brittle newspaper article picturing a teenage Granny Falkner
and her two sisters in gowns and upswept hairdos,
grinning. The headline read Dance Marathons a
Family Event for Sexton Sisters. Piper smiled in
delight as she read about her dancing grandmother
and two great-aunts, both of whom now lived in
Florida. Only a year separated the three sisters and
they were all still full of vinegar. Piper shook her
head and bit her lower lip. The Sexton sisters had
probably been the most sought-after women in the
then-thriving town of Mudville, Mississippi. They

had all married well and enjoyed enduring marriages.

Near the bottom of the box, beneath pressed corsages, a string of buttons and a small ring box of costume jewelry, Piper's fingers curled around a hardback book the size of a videotape. She withdrew it slowly, thinking the faded pink journal was possibly a diary or even a recipe book. But handwritten on the front in neat slanted script were the words *The Sexton Sisters' Secret Guide to Marrying a Good Man.*

Piper's eyebrows lifted in amazement, and she laughed softly. Gran and her sisters had conducted their own manhunt? An ancestral account to guide her on her mission.... Maybe there was hope after all.

## CHAPTER TWO

*Always wear clean gloves, since a marriageable man might reveal himself in the most unlikely of places.*

"'MORNIN', Piper. What's shakin'?" Lenny Kern bellowed from the porch of his mother's town house. He stood leaning against a post, picking his teeth, half-dressed and shiny, as if he'd been loitering long enough for the dew to have settled on him.

Piper, hoping to slink to her car unnoticed, acknowledged her neighbor without slowing. "Hey, Lenny."

"Whew-we! You look *goooooooooood.*"

His gaze swept her figure, pausing at her yellow silk blouse, and again at her knees extending from the snug, short black skirt. He grunted in appreciation and Piper briefly considered removing a too-tight high-heeled pump and bouncing it off his leering head.

"Did somebody die?" he asked, utterly serious.

"No," she said slowly, as if speaking to a child, "I'm going to work."

He shifted and scratched his hairy stomach, which protruded slightly over the waistband of his slept-in cutoff jean shorts. "You gotta work again today?"

She quirked an eyebrow and unlocked the door of her aged white minivan. "Yeah, Len, it's called gainful employment."

"But you must put in—" he looked heavenward and counted on his fingers for what seemed like an eternity, then turned wide eyes her way "—close to forty hours a week!"

"At least," she agreed wryly, opening the creaky door.

Lenny looked mournful. "I'm sorry for you, Piper. A woman like you shouldn't have to do nothin' but stay home and take care of her man."

As she swung into her seat, with one hand tugging on her hem, she swore under her breath. "Some girls have all the luck, I guess."

"Say, Piper, if you have an extra cake just layin' around the food lab for the flies to eat, bring it home this evening, would ya? It's Mom's birthday."

Striving to remain civil, Piper gripped the inside door handle and said, "You probably shouldn't count on it, Len. Why don't you order her something special?"

He snapped his fingers. "Good idea. I'll call the day-old bakery and see if they've got something that ain't too hard."

She smiled tightly, feeling a pang of sympathy for sweet old Mrs. Kern. "Good luck, Len." She closed the door and rammed the key into the ignition, her motions further hurried by the sight of Lenny loping off the porch and toward the van. He stopped and banged on the window, leaving large greasy fingerprints.

Reluctantly, Piper rolled down the window two inches. "I'm running late, Len."

He smoothed a hand over his uncombed raggedy mane of dark hair and grinned. He really wasn't a bad-looking man, he was just so...base. "Since I'm havin' Mom a party, why don't you come over for a piece of cake, say, oh, about seven? We'll watch 'Wheel of Fortune' together."

"I'll try to stop by and wish Margaret a happy birthday," she said pleasantly, nodding and rolling up the window at the same time she eased down the driveway.

"I'll get out my baby pictures!" Len yelled, trotting alongside the van until she cut the wheels, prompting him to jump back into the wet grass to prevent a crushed bare foot.

Piper heaved a sigh of relief as she pulled away, but guilt struck her when she saw Lenny's shoulders sag in her rearview mirror. After staying up late to read *The Sexton Sisters' Secret Guide to Marrying a Good Man,* she'd gone to sleep with a smile on her lips and determination in her heart to keep an open mind where Mudville men were concerned. But at the first sight of her persistent neighbor this morning, her mind had banged shut like a newly oiled door. And although she was a little more than positive that Lenny Kern did not hold the key to her destiny, she renewed her pledge to give every eligible man that crossed her path a fair assessment.

Low-hanging black clouds crowded the sky as she pulled into the nearly deserted parking lot of a video rental store to return three movies. It looked like rain for sure. Rain wasn't all that unusual for a summer day in Mississippi, but this one day, Piper had forgotten her umbrella. Still, perhaps a shower would alleviate some of the ever-present humidity, she thought hopefully.

Piper reached around to loosen her blouse from her sticky back and glanced at the movies in her hand with a faint pang of embarrassment. Was there a flick she hadn't seen? Black-and-white, Technicolor or colorized, romance, action or science fiction—she loved them all. For ninety minutes she could escape, finding a new life infinitely more interesting and fulfilling than hers.

It wasn't as though she didn't love her job as a food scientist—she *did*. And despite her good-natured complaints about living in a small town, she enjoyed the sense of community in Mudville. But she realized last night while reading the manhunting guide that although she'd spent years convincing herself she didn't want a man, she'd been fooling herself. She wanted her own happy ending, and as much as she hated to admit it, she wanted a loving companion by her side when the credits on her life rolled by.

She had just slid the tapes into a night drop box when a sound from the front of the store drew her attention. Henry Walden, owner of Videoville and town playboy, stuck his head out the door. "Piper Shepherd, is that you?"

Piper stared at the man who'd barely looked her way the five hundred or so times she'd been in his store. He had pale hair and tanned skin and seemingly row upon row of brilliantly white teeth. Henry wore his usual uniform of tight jeans, black pointed-toe boots and sleeveless shirt that showed off the tiger's-head tattoo on his left biceps. Although he looked to be in his mid- to late-thirties, he typically kept company with girls half his age. And twice her bra size.

Still, Henry was eligible, and handsome in a flashy kind of way. She remembered her pledge and smiled up at him. "Who does it look like, Henry?"

He seemed mesmerized by her legs. "I'm not sure—you look so…so…I've never seen you wear a dress."

Satisfaction and surprise warmed her. Were men so superficial that a simple change of clothes could elicit such a response? She was the same person she'd been yesterday, wearing drawstring khakis and an oversize T-shirt. Her scuffed clogs were substantially more comfortable than these toe-pinching pumps, so she was relatively sure she *looked* happier in her old clothes.

"Funeral?" he asked, utterly serious.

"No," she retorted. "Can't a girl dress up once in a while?"

He crossed his muscular arms and pursed his lips, surveying her as if he'd just made a discovery. "Absolutely," he said. "Listen, Piper, I've been meaning to call you and see if you'd like to go out sometime. What do you say?"

Not quite sure if he was asking her out or asking

her if he could ask her out, Piper nodded. "That would be nice...I think."

He nodded confidently, as if he expected no less than her acquiescence, and chewed on the inside of his cheek. A smile curved his fetching mouth as he studied her legs. The silence stretched between them until Piper felt as if she stood on two juicy drumsticks.

She gestured toward her van, which was still running. "Well, I guess I'd better be going."

Henry, nodding and chewing, watched her while she climbed inside awkwardly, aware of the expanse of thigh she revealed in the process. Embarrassment mixed with doubt and anticipation made her queasy as she drove away, and she suddenly remembered why she'd stopped dating in the first place—it hadn't been worth the strain. She'd barely begun her day, and she was already exhausted. Still, she was making progress. She had the *threat* of a date anyway.

More out of habit than necessity, Piper slowed at the caution light before proceeding onto Patty Richards Kegley Boulevard, the main thoroughfare of town. Twenty-two years ago Patty Richards Kegley had made the mistake of stepping out onto what had then been called Main Street in front of the single Mudville fire truck as it rushed to a grease fire at the drive-in on the far end of town. For her misfortune, she'd been immortalized in street signs, and the drive-in had created a sandwich in her name. Piper hoped if she herself incurred a mortal wound within city limits, she would at least warrant an entrée.

The Mudville morning rush hour typically dragged on for a full fifteen minutes when nearly one hundred workers leaving the midnight to 7:00 a.m. shift at Blythe Industries food plant clogged Kegley Boulevard in a semimad dash for a window seat at either Tucker's Good Food Place or Alma's Eats. Piper avoided the tangle by timing her commute for seven-thirty, which gave her ample time for the ten-minute drive and a cup of coffee before she donned her lab apron at eight.

The rain started falling in sheets just as the company's familiar blue and gray concrete sign came into view. Blythe Industries lay long and wide in a carved-out section of woods about a mile outside of town, past Trim's Food Market, the new high school and the old car wash. Pure coincidence had landed her the job of chief food scientist when the plant opened a year ago. She'd been visiting her grandmother and they'd run into Mr. and Mrs. Edmund Blythe over apple oatmeal at Alma's. The businessman had been ecstatic to learn of Piper's educational and professional background and offered her a job on the spot. Not entirely thrilled with her position as a label-ingredient tester at a Biloxi packager, and eager to be near her aging grandmother, Piper had accepted. The money was better than average and she'd made quite a dent in her college loans, but she found it amusing that she, who was allergic to chocolate and averse to sweets in general, was in charge of creating many of the desserts ordered at fast-food restaurants all over the country.

She was glad to be starting a new project today, she decided as she circled the full parking lot searching for a vacant space, despite the fact that someone from the Bentley Group was arriving this afternoon to offer tips on the kind of dessert they were looking for. Working with a suit looking over her shoulder didn't rank high on her list, but if Bentley signed for a new dessert, Edmund Blythe had promised her a very handsome bonus, so she aimed to please. Plus, a new face would take her mind off her after-hours manhunting mission. Her nerve was dwindling rapidly.

Through thrashing windshield wipers, she spotted one wide parking space on the end of a row and headed toward it. Cursing the van's absence of power steering, Piper started turning well before the

spot to leverage a good angle. Out of the corner of
her eye, she saw a small black sports car dart
around the corner and wheel deftly into the spot.
Piper slammed on the brake, bouncing her forehead
against the unforgiving steering wheel and biting
her tongue. Pain exploded in her sinuses while stars
floated behind her eyes. And she had the vaguest
thought that the cut in her mouth would affect her
tasting abilities for the day. Damn pushy salesmen!
They bombarded the plant daily, trying to coax Edmund Blythe into using their branded ingredients in
the desserts produced on the line.

She pressed her hands against her forehead,
blinking back involuntary tears. A low thumping
noise invaded her senses and she realized someone
was knocking on her window. Loath to move her
pounding head, Piper glanced up slowly to see a
man standing outside beneath an umbrella, peering
in at her. He wiped away the rain on the glass, then
yelled, ''Are you all right?''

Her first instinct was to fling open the door and
send the stranger sprawling, but her head hurt so
much, she could only nod. He knocked again and
motioned for her to lower the window. She cranked
down the glass gingerly, giving him the same two
inches she'd allowed Lenny this morning.

However, if she hadn't been so angry, she would

have appreciated the fact that the stranger was a measurable improvement over Lenny. His dark hair was cleanly shorn and he was wearing a shirt—a dress shirt, no less—and a tie, which was reason enough for pause in these parts. His clear eyes were the color of the rain dripping from his umbrella and topped with dark eyebrows, which were drawn into a vee. "Are you all right?" he demanded again.

Furious at her physical response to the nitwit, she swallowed a mouthful of blood and narrowed her eyes at him. "You," she said thickly, "are a menace."

The man's eyebrows shot up and he pulled back a few inches. "Me?" he sputtered. "What about you? Don't you know you're supposed to have your lights on when it's raining?"

Piper licked her lips, testing her tongue. "I didn't expect," she said, her voice escalating with each word, "anyone to be driving like a maniac *in the parking lot!*" She winced at the pain and exhaled.

"It's a good thing you had your seat belt on," he snapped.

"It's a good thing I'm not carrying a gun," Piper returned.

He scowled, gesturing. "Are you all right or aren't you?"

"I'll live," she muttered, fingering the goose egg fast forming on her forehead.

"Look, give me a minute to move my car," he said. "You can have the parking space."

"Don't do me any favors," she said dryly.

"I didn't see you," he said tersely, "or I would have gladly let you have the spot." He strode toward his car, shielded by the umbrella. His movements were jerky as he unlocked the door and lowered himself inside. Within a few seconds, he had backed out of the spot and disappeared around the corner.

Piper eased into the space, her heart still racing from the encounter. After she turned off the engine, she leaned forward and rolled her eyes up at the sky, hoping for a few minutes' reprieve to make the dash into the building. When none seemed forthcoming, she fished a plastic grocery bag out of the glove box. After tying the handles under her chin, she took a deep breath, then shot out of the door into the unrelenting cloudburst.

She didn't make it far. Her pumps didn't have the same grip as her trusty clogs. One second she was jumping puddles, the next she was flat on her back on the pavement, completely winded and half-submerged, her head held out of the water, she suspected, by the knot rising swiftly on her crown. She squeezed her eyes shut against the pain. Mercifully the rain suddenly stopped.

"You're accident prone," a male voice said above her.

Piper opened her eyes slowly to see the salesman kneeling over her, his umbrella providing the imagined lapse in the downpour. She considered the depth of the puddle—surely drowning would be less painful than dying of humiliation.

"Are you all right?" He grasped her arm and pulled her to her soggy feet, but she felt off balance and leaned heavily on his arm.

"I should have let you keep the parking spot," she murmured, still a little fuzzy, and very, very wet. Water streamed off her clothes, which were seemingly vacuum-packed to her backside.

"Do you feel well enough to walk?" he asked, his breath fanning her face as they huddled under the umbrella.

Piper conjured up a smirk. "What are my options?"

"I could carry you," he said simply, one side of his mouth drawing up into a lopsided smile.

Her heart lodged near her throat at the prospect and time stood still for an instant. His gaze locked with hers and Piper swallowed painfully. They might have been captured in their own little snow globe, separated from the rest of the world by some transparent barrier. Rain drummed on the umbrella and water ran around their feet. Piper's tongue felt thick, but she wasn't sure if it was swollen from biting herself or if she'd suffered brain damage from the combined knocks to her head.

"N-no," she stammered. She would already be the laughingstock when she walked into her office—she'd never live it down if she arrived high in the arms of a stranger. "I'll walk."

"That might be difficult." He shifted and fighting a smile, he held up the heel to one of her pumps.

Her heart sank. "I'll crawl," she amended.

"Come on," he urged, turning her toward the building. "I owe you one."

"You certainly do," Piper said briskly, but his throaty chuckle relaxed her slightly. He bore more of her weight than she did as they made their way across the short walkway and up a sweeping set of limestone steps. Piper's vital signs went haywire and she fluctuated between wanting the encounter to end and wishing for another lap around the grounds on the arm of this man.

His driving skills aside, *this* was a man worth hunting. Tall, solidly built from what she could see, nice dresser. Piper frowned. He obviously was not from Mudville—hmm, that could be a problem. Still, she was thrilled that she'd managed to stumble over such a prize specimen so early in her hunt. Phrases from her grandmother's guide popped into her head and she searched for something brilliant to say that would erase the impression she'd given him.

But her romantic musings came to a screeching halt when she glanced down at his left hand. Winking back at her, mocking her from his third finger was a very gold, very sparkly, very substantial-looking wedding band.

Her quarry had been bagged by someone else.

Piper suddenly felt cold, wet and miserable. Even if she did need the practice, she wasn't inclined to waste her fledgling feminine wiles on a married man. She set down her foot wearing the good shoe on the top step, then felt the rain-soaked heel snap off. The pain in her ankle surpassed any of the injuries she'd received in the last fifteen minutes. She howled, her dignity long gone.

Ian felt his clumsy companion lurch sideways, and bent his knees to accommodate her weight, such as it was. His flash of irritation was replaced by concern at her high-pitched yelp. At least they had progressed to an overhang, so he abandoned the umbrella to clasp her other arm.

"My ankle, my ankle, ow, ow, ow," she whimpered, holding her right foot off the ground. With the white plastic bag tied around her head, her shimmering eyes and her drenched, dripping clothes, she looked pitiful.

"Hold still," he said, bending to lift her into his arms.

"No," she protested, pushing at his chest with laughably tiny hands.

"Hold still," he insisted, swinging her up, "before you break your little neck." She gasped with indignation. Ian pressed his lips together and stared straight ahead. He concentrated on the few remaining steps into the building to keep his mind off the fact that his hands were full of very attractive woman. The "little" had just popped out. Petite and elflike, she could be anywhere between her early twenties and mid-thirties. But she had a mouth like a teenager, and seemed just as flighty.

If Blythe Industries was riddled with ditzy employees, maybe he should rethink their business liaison. Perhaps this project would be better off in the hands of the midsize food plant he worked with in Peoria.

"I can walk, thank you." She moved against him, struggling like a soaked kitten.

Glancing at her was a mistake—he nearly stumbled when he looked into her eyes. Pale blue, virtually black around the edges, and brimming with anger. Childlike long lashes. Chiseled, small features, with dark, spiky hair sticking out from under her makeshift rain bonnet. And her wet wriggling was doing things to his body. "We're almost there—you're making things worse," he said tightly. *Much worse.* He'd come to Mudville hoping to forget about women for a while, and within hours of arriving, he already had his hands full...literally.

He dragged away his gaze to look around for someone to open the double doors heralding the entrance to Blythe Industries, but no one else was in sight. Thankfully, the doors slid open automatically.

About two dozen people loitered in the two-story lobby, talking, waiting for the elevator, stamping the rain from their feet onto pale marble tile. A few people drifted in through another entrance, directly opposite the one he and Miss Mishap had chosen. A tall desk sat unattended in the reception area. He looked around for a place to set down his load, and moved toward a small cluster of couches and chairs.

Meanwhile, his load was caterwauling, "Put... me...down!"

A few heads turned at the obvious distress in her

voice, and his irritation flared. How like a woman to bite the hand trying to feed her.

"Be quiet," he snapped, "before I drop you on your wet backside." Indeed, the going was precarious with all the water dripping from her onto the slick floor.

She refused to behave. Still pressing against his chest, she shouted, "Put me down!"

He did. Ian dropped her unceremoniously onto the most absorbent-looking couch in the lobby. She bounced twice on her behind, arms flailing, eyes angry.

"There," he pronounced, removing a handkerchief to wipe his own hands. His wet suit sleeves and the front of his shirt, however, were beyond patting dry.

"Thank you," she said with a clenched jaw, trying to sit up. She reached forward to massage her ankle, which had already begun to swell. Despite her ungrateful attitude, Ian winced in sympathy. She needed medical attention.

A stout, middle-aged man broke from the staring crowd at the elevators, his stride purposeful. Ian recognized Edmund Blythe from the meetings in Chicago, where they had signed a sizable contract. "Piper, is that you? Good Lord, what happened?"

In wet stocking feet, the woman he called Piper

looked up from the couch. She tore off the plastic bag, revealing choppy short, dark hair. Only someone with her incredible bone structure could have carried off the minimal hairstyle. "Good morning, Edmund." She rolled her eyes toward Ian. "I was told that I'm accident prone."

The man turned to Ian, then his face lit up in surprise. "Well, Mr. Bentley! I wasn't expecting you until this afternoon, but it's good to see you."

Ian took the beefy hand Edmund proffered. "Hello again, Mr. Blythe. I suppose I was anxious to see your operation firsthand."

"And oversee the creation of your new dessert," Mr. Blythe added with a knowing smile.

Relenting with a nod, Ian said, "This is an important project."

Blythe grinned. "That's why we have our chief food scientist ready to begin work on your assignment today—under your supervision, of course."

"I'm impressed with the quality of my Italian restaurants' desserts. I'm anxious to meet him."

Ian hadn't meant to ignore the wet bundle he'd carried into the building, but he was eager to get on with business. At the sound of her clearing her throat rather loudly, though, he glanced down to find her staring at him, wide-eyed.

"Her," she said, smirking.

"I beg your pardon?" Ian asked.

"The chief food scientist," she said, still smiling. "It's a her." She slung moisture off her small hand and shoved it toward him. "Piper Shepherd, accident-prone chief food scientist, at your service."

# CHAPTER THREE

*Don't waste precious time dallying with ne'er-do-wells, drunks, married men and other undesirables.*

IAN BLINKED. The clumsy little pixie who couldn't maneuver her way from the parking lot into the building was in charge of the most important project on his drawing board? He took the damp slender hand she extended and gave it a light shake, lest he injure another part of her body—a part she would need for cooking. "My apologies," he offered, feeling a flush climb his neck. "I'm Ian Bentley."

"So I gathered," she said, smiling tightly. "Looks as though we'll be working together, Mr. Bentley."

From the expression on her face, Ian made a mental note to keep tabs on the butcher knives in her food lab. Flustered, he wasn't sure what to do or say next. Thankfully, Edmund stepped in.

"Piper, let's get you to the infirmary so the nurse can take a look at your ankle." His face creased in concern. "And that bump on your head." He clasped her arm and eased her to her feet. She glared at Ian, as if daring him to offer to help so she could take off his head. Instead, feeling absurdly responsible, he collected her dismembered shoes and followed them. Edmund bent at the waist to aid his petite patient, and Piper hopped on one foot, leaving a trail of water that dripped from her shrunken hem.

People stared at him with accusing eyes as they traipsed through the lobby, as if he'd run her down in the wet parking lot. He averted his gaze from her round behind, but the glimpse of thin bra straps through the back of her transparent blouse seemed even more provocative, so he settled for staring at his own black tassel wingtips as they walked to the elevator.

"Mr. Blythe, perhaps Mr. Bentley would be more comfortable waiting in your office," Piper suggested, turning those incredible eyes his way.

Her tone sounded deceptively generous, but Ian suspected she actually wanted to be spared his company. The knowledge roused the perverse desire in him to remain close by. "I may be a menace, Ms. Shepherd," he said with a slight smile, "but I'm a concerned menace. I'll tag along, if you don't mind."

Her mouth tightened, but she nodded curtly.

Edmund Blythe looked at him, then her. "What exactly happened, Piper?"

Ian opened his mouth to take full blame, but she cut him off. "Mr. Bentley saw me fall in the parking lot and he…came to my rescue."

Surprised, Ian lifted an eyebrow. Of course, she was supposed to be winning him over.

"Mighty nice of you, Bentley," Edmund declared, holding open the elevator door when it arrived. She limped in ahead of him, on her boss's arm. If Ms. Shepherd's skirt dried molded to her backside, Ian knew his attention span would be seriously compromised for the remainder of the day.

Just as the doors started to close, an intercom crackled. "Mr. Blythe, please come to your office. Mr. Blythe, please come to your office."

Edmund frowned and blocked the door from closing with one stout arm while supporting Ms. Shepherd with the other. "Sounds like I'm needed upstairs. Can you manage, Bentley?"

Startled, Ian nodded and moved hesitantly toward a wide-eyed Ms. Shepherd, whom Edmund passed over to him as if she were a slim runner's baton. Then her boss strode out of the elevator, and the doors slid closed, shutting out curious onlookers as they craned for a better look.

They stood in silence for several seconds, he holding on to her arm awkwardly and she alternately leaning into and away from him, as if she couldn't make up her mind. She was a small woman, of average height, but as delicate-looking as a doe. She'd probably broken her ankle falling off those ridiculous shoes. A bit irritated, Ian marveled at how different the day was turning out to be than he'd imagined. At this rate, they'd never get any work done.

Which would delay his return to Chicago, he suddenly realized, and smiled.

"You can let me in on the joke later," she said, wobbling, "but for now I'd settle for you pushing the basement button."

He sobered and, since his fingers were full of her shoes, pressed the button carefully with a knuckle on his right hand, setting them into motion. Tension crackled in the few cubic feet of air. Ian felt at a loss to explain how rapidly they'd gotten off on the wrong foot, but if he'd learned anything in his bachelorhood, regardless of fault, it was the man who was expected to make amends. He cleared his throat, then said, "I have to admit I underestimated Mudville—is every morning around here this exciting?"

"Oh, yeah," she said as the bell dinged and the

doors opened. "You should have seen the commotion on Main Street when Alma ran out of biscuits last Tuesday at her restaurant."

He laughed and helped her out onto the smooth tiled floor of the basement, but she promptly slipped. Ian caught her in what resembled a low waltz dip, slamming their bodies together and bringing their faces within inches of each other. She gasped and he could feel her heart pounding. Desire surged through his body, surprising him. Her eyes grew large and startled. Her skin shone translucent, dewy from the downpour, her cheekbones high and her mouth rounded in an O. A schoolboy urge to kiss her flooded him, but overwhelming the various signals his body transmitted was the screaming pain in the third finger on his left hand. Meredith's ring felt like a sharp, metal tourniquet.

"Ms. Shepherd," he said in a low voice as he pulled them upright in slow motion and tried to shake off the attraction he felt for her. "It seems that you're determined to fall again. Our progress would be quicker if you would allow me to carry you the rest of the way."

She straightened her slender shoulders and adopted a haughty look. "Oh, you're asking this time?"

He pursed his lips, considering the wisdom of

arguing with her. The woman was a confounding mix of spunk and vulnerability. Her arrogance annoyed him—he was only trying to help, and she continued to be difficult. Still, he recognized the dangerous signs of physical attraction, and the last thing he needed was yet another woman to complicate his life. Delivering Ms. Shepherd to the infirmary and putting distance between them struck him as the best solution. "I'm asking," he said with as much control as he could muster.

A look of defeat passed through her eyes and pink tinged her cheeks. "Well, um, since we only have a little farther to go…" Her voice trailed off and she nodded down a tunnel-like hallway.

Anxious to get her to the infirmary and take his leave, Ian bent and once again swept her into his arms. This time she didn't squirm or wiggle, but held herself stiff and unmoving instead. As if by mutual consent, they both stared in the direction of their destination. Ian quickened his pace and lengthened his stride until he reached a doorway over which a hanging sign announced Infirmary.

The infirmary was little more than a large closet containing a cot and tall metal cabinets with glass doors, behind which were arranged an impressive array of bandages and over-the-counter medications. As Ian lowered Piper onto the cot, an inner door that read Janet Browning, R.N. opened, and a woman sporting a pink smock, braces and big red hair emerged. "Good grief, Piper, what happened to you?"

"I fell and twisted my ankle."

The nurse leaned over and smoothed back her patient's hair. "Did you hit your head on the way down?"

"Sort of."

"What are you doing so dressed up anyway?" the nurse asked, impatience clear in her voice.

Ian bit back a smile and placed Piper's shoes on the cot next to her. Had Ms. Shepherd wanted to impress him? He glanced at her flushed face, then remembering his getaway plan, he stepped back toward the door. His neck felt sticky—damn, but it was humid in Mississippi!

He fingered his collar impatiently, and Meredith's ring pinched the inside of his knuckle. Biting back a salty curse, he twisted the band into a more comfortable position. If he didn't know better, he'd swear the thing was tighter than yesterday. This was definitely one of those times when being left-handed was problematic—and he'd never liked wearing jewelry, so the ring felt doubly cumbersome.

The nurse had lifted Ms. Shepherd's leg to inspect her ankle, giving him an inadvertent peek directly up her damp skirt. Under her nude hose, she wore red panties. Ian swallowed painfully and fought the urge to bolt without a word. "I'll...I'll be in Mr. Blythe's office if you need—"

"Thank you, Mr. Bentley," she cut in, smiling up at him from the cot. "I'm fine."

He glanced over her one last time, from her droopy, wet hair to her plastered clothing to her plump ankle. Ms. Shepherd was as opposite to Meredith as a woman could be. She was a total mess, but she couldn't have been more correct—she was very, very fine. Ian felt his body harden involuntarily. He nodded curtly, wheeled and fled for his wife, er, *life*.

PIPER SAGGED with dismay. Mortification washed over her as she gazed at her shredded panty hose and fat ankle. The man must have thought she was a complete nincompoop. Her immediate financial success—and her chances of being able to afford her grandmother's house—depended on impressing Ian Bentley. So far the only impression she'd made was the one she'd left in the parking-lot pavement.

"Boyfriend?" Janet Browning asked with one red eyebrow in the air.

Piper gave her a dry smile. "Hardly. He's Ian Bentley, our largest customer."

"He's a looker, girlfriend."

"He's okay," Piper relented. "But he's also my boss for a few days."

"Planning to put in a little *overtime?*"

Remembering the thrill of being carried in his arms, Piper masked her disappointment with indignation. "You're a nut. Didn't you see his wedding ring?"

Her friend scoffed. "Ring, schming. You take what you can get in this barren little town. Let's take a closer look at your ankle." Janet leaned over and pulled a small stool forward on which she propped Piper's swollen foot. She knelt and touched the flesh gingerly while Piper grimaced and sucked air through clenched teeth.

"I don't think anything's broken, but you've got a bad sprain. I can give you an anti-inflammatory. You should be back to work in a few days if you take it easy."

Alarm bolted through Piper and she sat up straight. "But I'm starting a new project today."

"With Mr. Bentley?"

"Yes."

"Can't Rich take care of it?"

Piper fought to keep from wrinkling her nose.

*She* was going to get that bonus, not her assistant. "It's not what you think—I have other reasons for heading up this project."

Janet smiled knowingly. "Admit it, Piper, working with Mr. Bentley is the reason you're dressed like a mannequin."

"Wrong," Piper replied calmly, loath to confess the embarrassing details of the manhunt that had unwittingly gotten her into this humiliating situation. "I knew someone was coming from the Bentley Group, but I had no idea it was a man or what he looked like."

"Oh, right," Janet said, her hands on generous hips. "So I guess you expect me to believe you've turned over a new leaf and are now dressing like you give a damn about men in general?"

Piper stuck her chin in the air. "Well, what if I am?"

"Then you're failing miserably."

As if she needed to be reminded. "Thank you, Dr. Ruth. Just wrap my ankle, will you?"

Janet walked to the cabinet and removed a roll of bandage, scissors and tape. "Lose the panty hose." She grinned, flashing her braces. "Bet you haven't heard that for a while."

"I'll ignore that remark."

"Hey, has your grandmother sold her house yet?"

"No, but she's moving this weekend."

"What a gorgeous place—those columns! I'd love to have it."

Silently, Piper agreed with her. Her grandmother's house resembled a miniature plantation, two high-ceilinged stories of limestone, with grand round columns studding the deep, wraparound porch. But the beauty on the outside couldn't begin to compare with the beautiful memories inside. The house represented all the good things about family that Piper had never been exposed to in her own home, and she wanted to own it more than anything. Which was why she needed to come up with something fabulous for Ian Bentley's coffeehouses.

A few minutes later, her wrapped ankle feeling much stronger, Piper made her way back to the elevator and up to her office where experience in the food lab had taught her to keep an extra change of clothes.

"What happened to you?" her assistant, Rich Enderling, asked when she walked into her office.

"Don't ask."

"Okay," he said slowly, scrutinizing her bare feet and wrapped ankle. He shrugged his wide shoulders and held up his hands in submission.

Ironically, auburn-headed Rich was one of the better-looking men in town. Rich had admitted to her his homosexuality a few weeks after joining Blythe, but revealed he hadn't yet decided to live an openly gay lifestyle. The fact that he'd come to Mudville to buffer his attraction to men spoke volumes for the selection. "Piper, don't forget, someone is coming this afternoon from the Bentley Group to talk about the new dessert."

She gave him a wry smile as she passed him on her way to her storage cabinet. "Thanks for the reminder." After opening the cabinet, she removed clean jeans, a white T-shirt and a navy blazer, plus red canvas tennis shoes.

"Uh, Piper?"

She turned. "Yeah, Rich?"

He gestured to her clothing. "Did somebody die?"

Smiling sweetly, she slammed the cabinet door. "Yes—the next person who asks me that question."

Piper marched into the ladies' room, and came to a toe-stubbing stop in front of the full-length mirror. Her mouth dropped open in horror. Her hair alternately stood on end and lay flattened to her head, her clothing hung wrinkled, spattered and damp. Mascara flecked her cheeks. And her ankle looked huge.

It was a good thing Ian Bentley was married—she'd never stop kicking herself if she thought she'd met an eligible man in her current state. She changed clothes and repaired her hair and makeup as best she could, glad when she could feel the painkiller Janet had given her kick in. She considered flushing the broken pumps down the toilet, but settled for slamming them into a metal trash can. Darn shoes! She'd paid a fortune for them years ago for *somebody's* wedding and hadn't worn them a half-dozen times since. Damn the man who invented these things! It was probably the same guy who invented panty hose.

She half limped, half stomped back to her desk and stuffed the ruined clothes into a plastic bag, snatched a clean lab coat from the cabinet and hobbled down the hall to the food lab. She'd planned to spend the morning whipping up two or three experimental desserts for the Bentley Group representative. Now she'd probably have to do it all with him looking over her shoulder—if her appearance and behavior hadn't spooked him into leaving altogether.

"Here she is now," Edmund said, his arms out to her and his face wreathed in smiles. A large room lined with counters, sinks and huge industrial-size stainless-steel appliances, the lab suddenly looked crowded with her boss, her assistant and her nemesis lined up against a counter, enjoying coffee and a sampler of Danishes and sweet breads from the production line.

"Hi, Edmund, Mr. Bentley."

She made brief eye contact with Ian. He acknowledged her with a nod, but his gaze swept over her, head to toe. Piper tingled, but vowed to maintain the most professional demeanor possible. He had removed his jacket and loosened his tie and top shirt button. Gorgeous, the man was simply *gorgeous,* she bemoaned inwardly, but recalled the nononsense advice from her grandmother's book. The man was off-limits, out-of-bounds, inaccessible and just plain taken.

Holding a mug in one hand and a slice of strawberry-cream-cheese-pecan-nut-bread in the other, he looked like most men when they ate—content. She wondered briefly if his wife was a good cook, then chastised herself. What did she care?

"How is your ankle?" he asked politely.

"Much better, thanks." She limped over to the coatrack, removed her blazer and donned the comfortable lab coat.

"I gave Mr. Bentley a tour of our facilities," Edmund announced.

"I see you raided the production line," she teased. "Enjoy your breakfast, gentlemen. I'll gather my supplies for the day."

"Piper, these caramel doughnuts are the most wonderful things I've ever tasted," Edmund declared, wiping a corner of his mouth. "If Harriet knew I was eating these, she'd have my hide." He shook his head and grunted.

She smiled at her boss, knowing he was laying it on thick for the sake of their guest. "Your secret is safe with me, Edmund." She noticed Rich studying Mr. Bentley unobtrusively and started in surprise.

Her assistant glanced her way, flushed, then straightened. "Speaking of having someone's hide, Prickett will have mine if I don't help with the morning inspection." He headed for the door, adding over his shoulder, "I'll check in with you later, Piper."

"Well, Mr. Bentley," Edmund said, wiping the sugar from his hands, "I'll leave you in the very capable hands of Ms. Shepherd."

Stepping into the deep supply closet kept her from hearing Mr. Bentley's response, only the muffled sound of his deep voice. The voice of a con-

fident, rich, successful, powerful man. Despite her
vow, she couldn't argue with the fact that her hands
shook and her heart raced at the thought of spending the next few days with Ian Bentley, ring or no
ring. Which simply demonstrated how desperate
she was, she realized with disgust, trying valiantly
to concentrate on the task at hand.

Tall shelves crammed with nonperishable ingredients towered over her—white sugar, brown sugar,
powdered sugar, white flour, bread flour, wheat
flour, baking soda, salt, dark cocoa, white cocoa
butter, peanut butter, assorted nuts, marshmallow
creme, fudge sauce, caramel sauce, strawberry
sauce, raspberry sauce and an exhaustive list of
other goodies. The fragrance alone tickled every
taste bud in her mouth, and simply inhaling was
worth a good fifty calories or so.

She gathered a handful of spices and flavorings
and tossed them into a sturdy metal cart, which
doubled as a step stool, along with five pounds of
flour and five pounds each of white and brown
sugar. She had several ideas, but she knew her banana-cream pudding would knock Mr. Bentley's
socks off.

Her train of thought led her to imagine other ar-
ticles of his clothing being knocked off, but she
immediately put on the brakes and reviewed nec-

essary ingredients in her head. So absorbed was she with her mental shopping list that when she heard his voice behind her, she froze.

"My, my, there are all kinds of tempting things in here."

Piper squashed down erotic thoughts, steeled herself and turned. Her pulse jumped at the sight of him leaning against the doorjamb, arms crossed over his broad chest. She managed a shaky smile. "Pick something you like and I'll add it to the cart."

His smile was slow and pulse-pounding. "Well, Ms. Shepherd, I wouldn't stop you from climbing on."

# CHAPTER FOUR

*Once you find a marriageable man, don't wink, tease, flirt or otherwise let him know you're interested.*

PIPER SQUEEZED a plastic bottle of banana syrup so hard, the top blew off and ricocheted between the metal shelving twice before rolling to a stop by the toe of her shoe. She replayed Ian Bentley's words in her mind. "Excuse me?" she asked, buying time. After all, she didn't want to make a fool of herself—either way—if she hadn't heard him correctly.

Mr. Bentley straightened, cleared his throat and pointed to her injured foot. "If you need to take the weight off your ankle, feel free to take a seat on your cart. I'm in no hurry."

His gray eyes were innocent, and Piper felt weak with relief. The mild painkiller was playing tricks on her. "Oh." She bent to retrieve the wayward lid. "No, I'm fine," she lied. Fingers of pain probed her ankle even as she loitered in the closet, lusting after an unavailable man. Determined to focus on her bonus, Piper stood erect and replaced the lid on the bottle. The provocative shape of the hand-friendly, tapered container made her nervous, so she deposited it abruptly into the cart. "I—I hope you like the recipe I have in mind for your new dessert, Mr. Bentley."

He shrugged and glanced around the room. "You're the expert. And I'll eat just about anything sweet…unless it contains bananas."

Piper stopped and stared. "Bananas?"

He nodded. "I like them, but unfortunately, I'm allergic."

"Allergic," she parroted. "Imagine that."

His wide shoulders rose in a shrug. "And I have to admit—anything chocolate is bound to get my attention."

"Chocolate," she repeated, already picturing the hives, the swollen eyes and the thick tongue she'd develop from all the tasting. "That's…great. Nobody does chocolate like I do chocolate." *Reluctantly.*

He grinned, looking boyish and outrageously appealing. "Terrific. Of course, if you feel compelled to make something with bananas, go ahead."

"But you just said—"

"I don't believe in depriving the buying public simply because I can't indulge. I try my best to ignore cravings for things I shouldn't have."

Piper gazed into his eyes and swallowed. Was he referring to this, this...*attraction* between them and his status as a married man? Or was she reading too much into his words because of her own sudden awareness? "I wouldn't want you to, um, suffer."

His eyes darkened and he leaned toward her almost imperceptibly. "Some things are worth the consequences, no matter how dire."

Just as her knees weakened, the fluorescent light caught the glint of his wedding ring, sobering Piper. Even if the man wasn't taken, he emanated too much sexual energy for her comfort level. But under *no* circumstances would she become involved with a married man. A flush of embarrassment climbed her neck—she was so naive when it came to men that she couldn't even be sure if he was baiting her for an affair or simply informing her he'd break out in a rash if he ate bananas.

Thankfully, Mr. Bentley saved her from responding. He glanced away and drew himself up, breaking the moment—if indeed there'd been one. "I'm more interested in the aesthetic appeal of your recipes, the marketability and—" he smiled tightly "—the cost, of course."

Feeling like a ninny, Piper grabbed a canister of white and dark cocoa and added them to the pile. Then she gripped the cart handle with sweaty hands and headed toward the door. Her best hope to diffuse the sexual tension was to minimize their time together—she'd get rid of him as soon as possible and work overtime until the project's completion. He'd be on his way back to Chicago in no time, after he'd signed a contract for the most decadent chocolate dessert she could concoct, of course. "We can discuss the recipe in the lab," she suggested, frantic to get some distance from the man.

"Let me take that," he offered, reaching for the handle of the cart.

She glanced down to maneuver around Bentley's expensive-looking shoes. "That's all right—"

His fingers brushed hers, nudging her hand aside. For some reason, the touch seemed more intimate than either time he'd lifted her into his arms. She pulled away so quickly, she nearly threw herself off balance. Then she sidled past him as gracefully as she could with her clubby ankle, and indicated her favorite work counter, where he parked the cart.

Keenly aware of him following her, Piper crossed the checkerboard black-and-white tile floor to the coffeemaker. She poured herself a cup of black decaf coffee and refreshed his cup as well. Striving for nonchalance, she conjured up a smile. "Do you know how intimidating it is to serve coffee to a man who owns some of the most successful coffee-houses in the country?"

"I'm a simple man—I like my coffee black and strong." Bentley lifted his cup and took a deep swallow. "This is actually quite good."

Calmer now, Piper pointed toward the corner of the lab where a white rectangular table sat surrounded by six sterile-looking chairs. Her foot was beginning to throb and she needed to rest before pulling out the mixing bowls. "Let's sit and discuss the finished product."

Piper approached a set of tall file cabinets, opened a drawer, walked her fingers across tabs, then withdrew the thick folder she'd compiled on the Bentley Group. Slowly she made her way over to the table and stood awkwardly, shifting good foot to injured foot and back, waiting for Mr. Bentley to sit so she could situate herself as far away from him as politely possible. But he pulled out a chair for her on one side and she felt obliged to take it. Alarm struck her when he tugged on the chair directly next to her, but he simply smiled and indicated the seat with a nod.

"For your foot."

Feeling silly for thinking he meant otherwise,

Piper lifted her foot onto the chair. Mr. Bentley set his cup of coffee on the table and captured the seat across from hers. She withdrew a pad of paper and a pen from a drawer in the table, and opened the manila file. "Now then, will the coffeehouses be franchised under the current name?"

He sipped and nodded. "Talk of the Town Coffeehouse."

"And do you have a name in mind for the dessert?"

Mr. Bentley shook his head and splayed his hands. "I'd like to hear your ideas—you look like a contemporary consumer."

She shrugged and pursed her lips. "As much as one can be in Mudville, Mississippi, I suppose." Piper waited, hesitant to discuss her elementary-sounding ideas with a master food marketer. "Well..."

"Go on," he urged.

She took a deep breath and plunged ahead. "I visualize a large dessert, one that can be shared." When he didn't laugh, she continued. "A subtle, rich flavor that lends itself to an accompanying drink, but doesn't compete with exotic coffees." When he still didn't laugh, she continued. "Presented in a unique dish that will attract attention when it's served."

He brought his coffee to his mouth for another sip. His clear eyes were unreadable, but one eyebrow twitched as he mulled over her ideas. He had a slight cleft in his square chin that she hadn't noticed before, but it appeared when he pressed his lips together. Other details jumped out at her, details she'd been too self-conscious to notice when they'd been practically nose to nose. A small concentration of gray compromised his thick dark hair front and center—probably premature since he didn't look to be much past thirty-five. A tiny pale scar on his lower lip left her wondering about the injury.

To cover her blatant perusal, she blurted, "What do you think?"

His mouth quirked, then curved into a smile as he leaned forward. "I was about to ask you the same thing."

Her lips parted and humiliation washed over her. Was she forever destined to make a fool of herself in this man's presence? "I—I don't know what you mean."

His eyes danced. "Ms. Shepherd, I think I know why your other recipes have been so successful in my restaurants—you put a lot of thought behind them."

Relieved with the change of subject and ridiculously pleased at his praise, she sorted through the file folder until she found a menu for the coffee-house and ran a shaky finger down the dessert section. "You offer various cookies, muffins, sliced pie, sweet breads and Danishes—all are prepackaged, sold in individual servings and relatively inexpensive."

"And simple to store and serve," he said. "I don't want something too complicated to prepare in volume."

On firm business footing at last, she nodded. "Agreed. I foresee Blythe providing the base element, prepackaged in bulk, with the last-minute toppings—sauces, whipped cream, etcetera—being added at the coffeehouses."

"So far, so good."

Piper reached down to scratch her ankle through the bandage with the end of her pen. "What retail price point are you looking for?"

"To serve two?"

"A serving for two to three."

"Probably no more than five ninety-five, which means I need the prepackaged product and toppings for less than three."

Ms. Shepherd chewed on her lip, and Ian watched carefully. He was amazed he'd been able to concentrate on anything she'd said to this point, even though she had exhibited remarkable insight into what he was seeking. Gone was the opinion that this woman was ditzy—clumsy, intriguing and engaging, perhaps, but not ditzy.

Earlier this morning he couldn't wait to escape her company. Then he'd fretted about her ever since he'd left. He'd been so fidgety and distracted that Edmund and Ms. Shepherd's assistant probably thought he suffered from attention deficit disorder.

He'd simply been concerned for her well-being, he'd told himself. But he had to admit, he'd been more preoccupied with the way she looked in those loose-fitting jeans when she removed her jacket in the lab than with the bandage around her ankle or the scraped skin beneath her wispy dark bangs.

Ian sniffed danger. No matter how much he told himself he did not need the entanglement of a brief affair—and certainly not with a valuable vendor connection—he couldn't keep himself from eyeing every flat surface in the lab and gauging its sex-worthiness.

"We can do it," Ms. Shepherd announced.

He inhaled sharply into his cup, sucking hot coffee down his windpipe. Lapsing into a coughing seizure, he barked like a hoarse seal. Ms. Shepherd half rose from her chair, but he waved her down as reality sank in. While his mind had wandered off into Lustville, she was actually trying to resolve business issues. Ian cleared his throat and carefully swallowed another mouthful of coffee. "I'm sure you can do it," he croaked. "I'm sure Blythe can do it, I mean."

"Of course our production manager will have to have the final say," she said in a cautious tone, "but at least now that I know what cost range you're shooting for, I can begin working on the recipe specs. Mr. Blythe informed me we're not the only plant in the running for your business. If you don't mind me asking, what am I up against?"

Absurdly, Meredith flashed in his mind. Then he fast-forwarded through the delicacies he'd sampled at the Peoria plant. "Right now, a white chocolate mousse is the dessert to beat."

Her lips curved into a sly smile. "We'll see about that." She squinted and looked at the ceiling. "If all goes well, I should have a few samples by to-morrow."

Panic rose in his throat. "Tomorrow?" He'd counted on at least a week before going back to Chicago, back to Meredith—and *two* weeks sounded better all the time.

She steepled her small hands and looked adorably apologetic. "Sorry. Typically I'd work much faster, but I'm afraid my little accident is going to slow me down. I'm sure you're anxious to get back home, so I'll do the best I can."

"Take your time!" When she drew back in surprise at his vehemence, he added, "I wouldn't want you to push yourself, and I could use a few days of rest and relaxation anyway."

She laughed, a rich, sweet-sounding noise. "You certainly came to the right place for R and R, Mr. Bentley. You won't have any trouble finding absolutely nothing to do in Mudville."

She took his breath away. It scared and thrilled him at the same time. "Ian."

Her smile wavered. "Pardon me?"

"Call me Ian."

Her gaze darted away, then back. "Okay…Ian. C-call me Piper." She swung her foot to the ground and rose awkwardly, then extended her hand. "I'll meet you back here tomorrow afternoon…Ian. We'll have more to discuss at that time."

A clear dismissal…exactly what he needed. But the disappointment he felt shook him. The ring on his left hand scraped against the table as he pushed himself to his feet, squeezing his finger painfully. With his good hand, he reached across and shook hers, resisting the urge to pull her toward him. "Don't put in any overtime on my account, Piper."

Her pointed chin came up. For a second, he

thought he'd hit a nerve, then she smiled. "Blythe wants your business, sir, and so do I."

IAN STOPPED by Edmund's office to thank him for the tour, then exited the building and exhaled noisily. What a morning...and what a woman. He felt strangely drained and exhilarated at the same time—he couldn't remember a similar experience. It must be the altitude or the humidity or something environmental, he decided. Indeed, the rain had moved on, taking the clouds, but leaving a blanket of the most cloying humidity Ian had ever endured—and it was barely midmorning.

He loosened his tie, snagging the expensive silk with the increasingly irritating ring. Biting back a curse, he yanked the tie out of his shirt collar and stuffed it in a pocket, then slung his jacket over his shoulder. He fingered the heavy gold band and removed fuzz and fibers from the prongs of the setting, which had accumulated from getting caught on every fabric surface he came in contact with.

Frustrated anew at the way it weighed down his hand, he tried to twist the ring into a more comfortable position, but he could barely move it. Damn, it was tight! How on earth did one get used to wearing such an encumbrance? A frown pulled at his mouth. Of course, getting used to the ring was undoubtedly a negligible exercise compared to getting used to having a woman around permanently. Day in, and day out. Night after night, year after year, decade after decade…

Ian shivered in the Southern heat and shook off the disturbing line of thought. He had the rest of the day free, and intended to relax. Chicago, Meredith and his decision to accept or reject her proposal were far, far away.

Retracing his steps through the parking lot, he chuckled, remembering the morning's events. Piper Shepherd had turned out to be the most entertaining person he'd met in a long time, although he felt relatively sure she wouldn't take that as a compliment. Thoughts of her gamin good looks and slim figure taunted him, but this had happened to him once before. Ten years ago a woman he'd been dating had suddenly pressed him for a commitment. In his immaturity, he'd panicked and picked up the next attractive woman who had crossed his path, effectively ruining a perfectly good relationship. No, this time he was determined to make up his mind about his future without the distraction of a comely stranger.

He climbed into his rental sports car and headed toward the little motel where he'd registered last night. Funny how one's attitude affected their perception of day-to-day events. Last week, being cooped up in a tiny room without cable news or an extra phone jack for his laptop computer would have driven him nuts, but now…now he hadn't the slightest urge to retrieve messages which had undoubtedly piled up in his absence.

But old habits were hard to break, and he was waiting for word from a fellow restaurateur, Benjamin Warner. Together they were purchasing an antebellum house in Savannah, Georgia, and turning it into a Southern diner. Their offer had been accepted, and Ian had overnighted his friend the signed papers for the closing. He called his message service and sat poised by the phone with a pad of paper, dialing his way through two dozen messages.

The next to last message was from his partner, Ben, explaining the Savannah deal had fallen through because of site-restoration restrictions— they'd have to wait another eighteen months before appearing before the preservation board. Extremely disappointed, Ian phoned Ben and told him they'd keep their eyes open for another opportunity. He also checked in with his assistant, dictated a quick memo and returned three e-mail messages.

His stomach rumbling, Ian swapped his suit slacks for pressed chinos and rolled up the sleeves of his dress shirt, making a mental note to purchase some casual clothing. Then he pointed his car in the direction of downtown Mudville, hoping the daylight would reveal something more appealing than he'd seen last night on his late drive into town. He circled the downtown area, aware that his unfamiliar car turned heads. To his gratification, the light of day unveiled a quaint little town, unbelievably busy with bustling pedestrians and older cars.

Oh, sure, the aged buildings could use a coat of paint, but he found the flower boxes and ornamental concrete curlicues charming in a Mark Twain kind of way. He pushed down the thought that becoming familiar with the town would give him insight into the paradoxical resident, Ms. Piper Shepherd.

When he drove by the city municipal building, he stopped on a whim and procured a map of the area. Lunch forgotten, Ian spent the rest of the afternoon driving around the outskirts of the city limits, in and out of pseudo-subdivisions and family neighborhoods. The houses were neat and attractive, and the lawns generous. And the clotheslines—he loved seeing clotheslines full of sheets and jeans and baby clothes, a novelty to a man who had lived in high-rise apartment buildings for the last fifteen years.

Caught up in the heady feel of the countryside, he tuned in to a local radio station and caught a couple hours' worth of Little League scores, live-stock reports and elementary-school 4-H speeches. Around four o'clock he stopped at a Mom-and-Pop gas station in the middle of nowhere, bought a homemade ham-and-cheese sandwich and an ice-cold root beer, and accepted the elderly owner's invitation to "sit a spell" on the porch. During the next hour, two cars and three riders on horseback kicked up dust on the narrow road in front of the store as Ian extracted Mudville's history from wrinkly Zeke Samuels.

In addition to Blythe Industries, a paper-box manufacturer and a sewing factory provided the majority of jobs for the area. Surprisingly, next to tobacco, the most lucrative crop seemed to be farm-raised catfish. The fish farms fed several lakes in the area, which pumped lots of tourist dollars into the town.

Thinking he might indulge in a day of fishing before returning home, Ian asked for directions and set off toward the nearest lake. A germ of an idea took root when he drove up on a crowded parking lot full of cars with out-of-town license plates. After picking up a brochure, he drove around the area, keeping an eye open for choice lots and empty buildings or houses. He stopped occasionally to get his bearings and to scribble a few notes, the wheels in his head turning.

Just after five o'clock he happened upon a grand limestone house set in a white-fenced clearing, framed with towering evergreens. His heart pounded as he stepped from his car and it tripped double time when he spied the For Sale sign. There were no cars around, but he walked up on the porch and rang the doorbell several times. When no one answered, he shielded his eyes and peered through a naked window. Antique furniture lined the walls, carpets stood rolled on end, packing boxes littered the floor. Tall ceilings, hardwood floors and a massive fireplace—the place was amazing.

Ian jogged back to the car, pulled his cellular phone from the glove compartment and punched in a number. "Ben? It's Ian—you're not going to believe this house I found..."

"YOU LOOK like you're on the injured list, Piper." Pharmacy clerk Gary Purdue squinted down at her from behind the reading-glasses display. A former high school basketball star, Gary had warmed the bench in college while he failed four years of pharmaceutical studies, then returned to Mudville to work in his father's drugstore and coach peewee baseball. He reminded Piper of a celery stick and he always spoke in sports terms.

"Thanks, Gary." Her face felt puffy, her tongue tasted thick and she yearned to tear off her clothes and claw at her itchy skin. "I need an antihistamine, pronto."

He grinned and tucked a chin-length strand of blond hair behind his ear. "Did someone sneak chocolate into a recipe when you weren't looking?"

"Yeah—me."

A frown made his face seem longer and thinner. "You're kidding, right?"

"Nope. I've got a customer who likes cocoa, and I aim to please."

"You're a real team player, Piper."

She gave him a tight, itchy smile. "Rah, rah."

He walked around the front of the counter and chose two packages of pills from a shelf. "Janet Browning couldn't help you, huh?"

"The infirmary was already closed." She grinned sheepishly and hiked up her right jeans leg to reveal her wrapped ankle. "And I probably wore out my welcome there this morning. Got anything for the pain?"

Gary's eyes widened in alarm. "Time out!" He propelled Piper back into one of the "waiting" chairs and knelt in front of her.

"Gary—"

"Relax, Piper, I was almost a doctor."

She pressed her lips together and permitted him to examine her ankle as if he knew what he was doing.

"Looks like a bad, bad fracture," he announced.

"It's a sprain."

"Or a sprain," he agreed quickly, nodding. He stood abruptly and disappeared behind the dispensing counter where his father's eyes and balding head were barely visible. Mr. Purdue waved, and she waved back.

Piper leaned back into the chair and scratched her forearms furiously, wondering what would happen next. She felt bumpy and raw.

Gary sprang back into the room holding a paper cup of water. He handed her the cup and three pills. "Dad says take the pink ones for your allergic reaction, and the other one for your ankle."

Piper swallowed the pills in one gulp and pushed herself to her feet. "Thanks."

"Of course, you're not supposed to drive after you take the painkiller."

She stopped and stared at Gary. "Now *you're* kidding, right?"

"'Fraid not. Have you eaten?"

"No."

He looked at her considering. "It'll hit you in about fifteen minutes, thirty max."

Piper half closed her puffy eyes in frustration, fighting the urge to cry. She waved toward the over-the-counter allergy medicine. "Can you ring me up?"

Gary suddenly seemed fascinated with his size fifteen high-top sneakers. "If you can stick around for a few minutes while I restock the Odor Eaters, I'll be glad to drive you home." He glanced up and smiled shyly, triggering a memory of Janet saying that Gary and his longtime girlfriend had recently split up. He fidgeted. "Honest, Piper, you shouldn't be behind the wheel after taking that medication."

Piper's mind raced as she struggled for a graceful way to get out of the situation.

"Thanks, pal, but the lady already has a ride home."

Piper turned to see Ian Bentley standing at the end of the aisle, dressed country-club casual and holding a tube of toothpaste. He smiled at her, showing off his pearly whites.

## CHAPTER FIVE

*Always carry protection—such as hair spray or a nail file—in case a suitor makes untoward advances.*

GARY NARROWED his eyes at Ian. "Piper, do you know this guy?"

Completely dismayed at the lifting of her heart, Piper nodded. "He's a...a business associate of mine." Ian Bentley had invaded her thoughts so thoroughly since he left, her afternoon performance in the lab had been a comedy of errors. She couldn't remember when she'd tossed out more unusable batches.

Ian walked up to the counter, handed his purchase to Gary and withdrew his wallet. "I'm headed your way," he said, glancing at Piper. "I'd be glad to drop you off."

Since she was relatively sure he was lying, and since the idea sounded so appealing, Piper felt compelled to decline. "I don't think—"

"It's the least I can do to make up for this morning." He smiled, and her resistance began to crumble. Acutely aware of Gary watching them, Piper wet her lips. "But my van—"

"I'll drop it off when Dad and I close up," Gary offered eagerly, then slid his gaze back to Ian and lifted his chin. "That way I can check on Piper when I leave the keys."

"Problem solved," Ian agreed cheerfully, lifting his palms.

Since the arrangement seemed safely unromantic, and too tired, itchy and throbbing to argue, Piper relented with a nod. After all, it wasn't like either man was going to come on to her the way she looked now. She thanked Gary and handed over her keys. Stifling the urge to scratch her puffy face, she quickly paid for the antihistamine and preceded Ian out of the store.

"What happened to you?" he asked as she walked under his arm out the front door of the pharmacy. At nearly six-thirty, the temperature still hovered in the low nineties, and the humidity hung unrelenting.

Piper smirked. "I'm accident prone, remember?"

He frowned, peering at her face. Feeling a bit light-headed, Piper wondered how much more splotchy she'd become, then realized she was getting used to looking bad in front of Ian Bentley—not that it mattered.

Without stopping, he clasped her wrist and turned over her arm, revealing an expanse of red, bumpy skin. His touch heightened the tingly sensation skittering across her tender flesh. "You didn't get a rash from falling in the rain in the parking lot."

"It's just allergies," she said, pulling away her arm for a good scratch. "I'll be fine by morning." Despite the heat, Ian looked terrific in a long-sleeve shirt with the sleeves rolled up, and pleated khaki chinos.

She stopped and waited while he unlocked the passenger-side door of his rental car, setting into motion the muscles in his forearm. He was left-handed, she noticed. His wedding band glinted in the ebbing sunlight, the diamonds winking a reminder of his status. Her heart fell into an erratic rhythm. When he opened the door, she hesitated. "I'm counting on the fact that you're not a serial killer."

He snapped his fingers. "I *knew* there was something I left out of my introduction."

"I'm usually more careful than this," she explained lamely as she lowered herself into the leather seat.

Ian gave her a wry smile. "I'll bet you don't even lock your front door." He closed the door, and Piper watched him as he circled in front of the car. The man was absolutely too sure of himself.

"I'll have you know," she said when he opened the door and swung into his own seat, "that the front door to my house is safely secured." Then she smiled sheepishly. "It's the back door I leave unlocked."

The rumble of his laughter filled the interior of the car. "I'll file away that information for future reference," he said, his eyes crinkling at the corners.

His tone was teasing, but Piper gripped her paper bag of drugs tighter in her lap. The air hummed with tension, as if she didn't already feel prickly enough.

He started the engine. "Have you had dinner?"

"Uh, no. I was going to hit the drive-through on the way home."

"Which drive-through?"

She grinned and pointed left. "*The* drive-through."

Ian chuckled, then pulled onto Main Street and followed her directions the short distance to the fast-food restaurant. "Think I'll get a bite myself," he said.

"Where are you staying?"

"Little motel on the edge of town. Baker's?"

"Baxter's."

He nodded. "Right."

"Not exactly the Holiday Inn," she observed.

Ian shrugged. "Clean sheets, good mattress, nice stationery."

She'd expected him to put down the little motor inn, to put down the whole town. Piper almost hoped he would so she could dislike him. Then she stopped—since when had snobs become more unlikable than flirtatious married men? She shook her head to clear it and blamed her mental lapse on the medicine she felt filtering through her body like cool menthol. Food would slow down the absorption of the painkiller—not a bad idea at this point, despite her aching ankle.

He rolled down the window and ordered two burgers, fries and drinks, refusing her offer to pay, but handing her the bags of food to plunder while the cashier made change.

Still spoiling for an argument, she said, "I can't believe a big-city restaurateur is actually eating fast food."

Unfazed, he lifted himself out of the seat slightly

to return his wallet to his back pocket. "Don't forget, I own a few fast-food franchises myself."

*A few dozen,* she corrected silently. Piper dragged her attention away from the muscles flexing beneath the fabric of his pants. "I know, but I guess I never thought you'd actually eat at one of them."

He settled back into the seat and gave her a deadly grin. "You've been thinking about me?"

Red flags sprang up behind her eyelids. Sirens sounded in her ears. Determined to keep her cool, Piper pursed her lips and shoved a burger into his hand. "Instead of putting words in *my* mouth, how about putting this in *yours?*"

He winked good-naturedly and unwrapped his burger with one hand while steering with the other. "Where to?"

"I thought you were headed my way," she reminded him, placing an order of French fries within reach and settling their drinks into cup holders.

One side of his mouth jerked upward. "I am— as soon as you tell me which way that is."

Piper had to smile since he'd spared her from Gary Purdue's good intentions. "Left at the light, past the tire center, right at Ms. Gardner's house, right again at the school-bus turnaround—"

"Um, perhaps you can tell me as we go along," he cut in with a laugh. Ian took a sizable bite out of his burger, then pulled onto Main Street behind an old pickup truck with a bed full of hay and a half-dozen children. "Good burger," he said thickly.

She nodded slowly and exhaled in relief—disaster diverted. He felt the chemistry between them, too, but she had ultimate control, she kept telling herself. No matter how much he made her brain and body short-circuit, and no matter how much she needed that bonus, she would not—repeat, would not—become involved with a married man.

Glancing at his profile out of the corner of her eye, she bit into her burger with a vengeance, then stared straight ahead.

Lined up with their backs against the truck cab, the kids were all redheaded and obviously related. They grinned at Piper and Ian, then waved shyly. Her ill mood dissolved like sugar in water.

"Looks like a great place to raise kids," Ian observed.

Piper noticed he was thumbing his wedding ring while they waited for the light to turn. Did he have children? Probably, she thought, grabbing a fry.

"I suppose," she mumbled, feeling a little queasy. She always ate too fast—a bad habit developed in the lab.

"Did you grow up here?"

She shook her head as they began moving again. "No—I grew up in Westin, a few hours north. But I spent summers here with my grandmother, so I'm considered a native."

"Are your parents still in Westin?"

Piper sucked cola through a straw, then delivered her stock answer. "I don't have a father, but my mother lives near there." *Or wherever her current boyfriend wants to lie down.*

"And your grandmother?"

Just the thought of Gran lifted Piper's spirits. "She's still in Mudville." Gran would like Ian, Piper was sure. Oh, except for one little detail...

"You must be close to her."

"She's the reason I'm here," Piper admitted.

"Ah," he said, nodding. "The answer to the riddle."

"What riddle?"

He glanced over and made a clicking sound with his cheek. "What's a nice girl like you doing in a place like this?"

Certainly not the most breathtaking compliment she'd received, but his words affected her nonetheless. "Making desserts for you," she said, striving to keep the conversation light.

"Touché."

She busied herself by taking another fry. "Besides, Mudville isn't that bad.'' *Unless you're looking for a man.*

''Oh, I know—I've been exploring.''

She raised her arm and indicated where he should turn. ''And did you find us to your liking?''

He made the turn, then locked gazes with her. ''Let's just say I've been pleasantly surprised by my discoveries.''

Piper glanced back to the road and pressed a finger against her temple, as if she could reorder the thoughts being processed inside. The sexual draw coming from Ian across the console resounded almost tangibly. His faded aftershave tickled her allergy-stricken nose—she was quite sure an untimely sneeze would be forthcoming. A five o'clock shadow darkened his square jaw. The temperature of her crawling skin rose with every chest-expanding breath he took. Her heartbeat pounded in her ears.

''Feeling better?'' he asked, lifting his cup for a drink.

''Yeah,'' she lied. ''The food helped.'' Piper took another bite, forcing herself to chew slowly and breathe deeply. Hormones aside, she still had to win this man's business.

Then a terrible thought occurred to her. Did Ian Bentley make a habit of traveling around, using his leverage as a powerful customer to engage in ex-tramarital affairs? Did he expect her to sleep with him to get his business?

"You look like you're in pain."

She swung her head to the side to look at him, and managed a shaky smile. "Oh, well, I guess I'm tired."

"If your pharmacy buddy is correct, you shouldn't have any problem going to sleep." He wadded up his burger wrapper.

Piper held open one of the bags for him to de-posit the trash. She definitely felt woozy.

"He must be a good friend of yours," he re-marked.

"Who, Gary? I've known him for years."

"He knows where you live."

Was he fishing? Piper kept her gaze riveted on the road. "Turn here. Everyone knows where everyone lives in Mudville."

She folded two fries into her mouth and chewed during the uncomfortable silence. Finally Piper swallowed and asked, "So, Ian, how did you get into the restaurant business?"

Ian pursed his lips and shook his head, as if he had nothing interesting to share. "I started flipping burgers for gas money when I was sixteen. It didn't take me long to figure out who was making all the money. I worked my butt off, sacrificed things most teenage boys want and scraped together enough cash to put a down payment on a franchise of my own about the time I should have graduated from college.''

''You bought a franchise all by yourself?''

''Nope. My folks mortgaged their house to come up with the rest of the money, and I wasn't about to let them down.''

''I assume you repaid their mortgage,'' she said dryly.

He grinned. ''About six months later, then I bought them a new home in Daytona.''

Piper glanced heavenward in the darkening interior of the car. The man was gorgeous, intelligent, rich, hardworking *and* a good son. She'd known him one stinking day and he'd already displayed nearly all the desirable characteristics listed in her grandmother's manhunting manual. And who knew—naked, he'd probably get an extra check mark or two.

She inhaled sharply at the direction of her rambling, scrambled mind. ''Turn here.'' She pointed, her hand shaking. ''About a half mile down, mine will be the fourth town house on the right.''

He raised one dark eyebrow. ''A town house? In Mudville?''

"It's really an old shotgun-style house with a postage stamp–size yard."

"Shotgun?"

"The front door is in line with the back door," she explained, gesturing when the houses came into view. "The mayor's daughter bought an entire row and renovated them for rentals. Mine's the blue one."

"Nice," he commented as he slowly wheeled into her narrow driveway. "Very nice." Smiling, he leaned forward and peered out the window.

Strangely buoyed, Piper silently gave thanks for the weekends she'd spent planting purple petunias and yellow barberry shrubs around the foundation of the little house—despite having to endure Lenny's ghastly company every dirt-grubbing minute.

At the thought of her nosy neighbor, she slid her gaze to the porch next door. Deserted, thank God. She'd pay penance later by going over to wish Mrs. Kern a happy birthday…after she'd bathed in pink chamomile lotion, and before she gave in to the descending lethargy.

She started gathering up their trash. "Thanks for the ri—"

At the sound of the car door opening, she glanced up in time to see the driver-side door closing. Once again, Ian circled around the front of the car. Piper's stomach twisted. He opened her door and smiled, but his wolfish charm had fled. Instead he seemed...nervous. Which made *her* nervous.

"I'll walk you to your door," he offered politely, pulling the trash and her shopping bag from her arms.

Silently, but with her heart pounding, she got out of the car and led the way down the stepping-stone walk between her house and the Kerns', limping. "Gary has my keys," she reminded Ian over her shoulder. "I have to go in the back door."

"So you weren't kidding." His voice floated up to her in the falling dusk—earlier this evening due to the cloud cover.

Her laugh sounded apprehensive even to her own ears. "No, I wasn't kidding." Her ankle throbbed, her stomach churned and her skin burned. Piper walked the short distance to the back of the house, turned right, crossed the tiny patch of grass that masqueraded as her backyard, then climbed the four steps leading up to the rear door.

His leather-soled shoes padded lightly on the steps behind her, like a countdown. With her back to him, Piper opened the door and pushed it inward, then spun around with a wide smile to relieve Ian of his load. But whatever clever parting line had been on her tongue eluded her when her gaze met his in the near darkness. He stood on the next to last step, a good six inches below her, which put them nearly eye to eye, hand to hand, and mouth to mouth. They were close enough to see, touch... and kiss.

She sank her teeth into her lower lip to stave off a groan of sheer desire and reached out to empty his arms. With a half pivot, she deposited the bags on the counter just inside the door, then realized her mistake when she turned back: both of them now had empty arms. She crossed hers, giving herself a white-knuckled hug. "Thanks," she said, nodding, her smile just as tight as her grip on her arms. "Ian," she added, still nodding.

He remained silent, during which her mind played several versions of how this evening could end—and only one of them would allow her to face herself in the mirror tomorrow. She turned to step inside.

"Piper."

Was it a question? A statement? She wasn't sure, but the word *yes* was not going to pass her lips, so she simply turned back and raised her eyebrows, hoping he could see them in the shadow of the stoop covering.

"I'd like to kiss you right now."

Her tongue seemed glued to the roof of her mouth.

"Did you hear me?" he whispered, shifting forward slightly.

She meant to laugh, but the noise came out sounding like a sigh. Piper cleared her throat and tried again. "I think, Mr. Bentley, that my ears are the only part of me that doesn't itch or hurt."

"Of course," he said quickly, inclining his head. "I'll leave so you can rest."

At that moment, the light on the Kerns' back stoop came on, and Lenny himself stepped out. He stood about thirty feet away, with his hands stuffed into the front pockets of his camouflage pants. No shoes and no shirt. Piper felt half relieved, half loath to see him.

"Hey, Piper," he bawled. "What's shakin'?" He spit through his teeth into the grass below, then leveled a stare at Ian.

"Boyfriend?" Ian murmured, obviously amused.

"No," she said, exasperated. "Hey, Lenny."

"You still comin' over for cake? I found one with pink icing left over from the bowling banquet that got rained out."

Piper exhaled noisily. "Tell your mother I'll be there in a few minutes, Len, okay?"

"Okay." He didn't move.

"Go on, Len."

"Okay." He spit again, glared at Ian, then went inside.

"Turn out the light, Len," she called. A few seconds later, the light went off.

She looked at Ian and bit back a smile.

He grinned, too, shaking his head. Then his smile dissolved and she watched in slow motion as he reached up and pulled her against him. His mouth met hers, stealing her half-formed words of protest, his breath cool and sweet against her fevered tongue as his strong arms surrounded her.

Her knees buckled and she lost herself in his kiss, allowing herself to be swept away by the surge of adrenaline and desire. Longing struck her low and deep, warming the juncture of her thighs. She moaned and fell into him, pressing her body against the hard wall of his chest. But when she felt his erection hard against her pelvic bone, she froze. Her eyes flew open and she pulled back, splaying her hand against his chest.

His breathing ragged, he stared at her, still holding her loosely around the waist. "Piper—"

Sanity returned in a rush. Mortified, she stepped backward until she felt the hard wooden door against her shoulder blades. "Ian," she said, her chest heaving, "I can't do this."

A frown creased his forehead for a split second, then he shoved his hand into his hair and exhaled heavily. "Okay…but can I ask why?"

She pressed her lips together, her ire rising. "Why?" She crossed her arms. "Well, actually, two things come to mind."

He looked bewildered, inflaming her further. "Two things?"

"Two," she repeated through clenched teeth. "You're a valued customer of Blythe Industries…"

"And?" he asked, eyebrows high, obviously unconvinced that their business relationship posed a substantial barrier to a one-night stand.

"*And?*" White-hot anger cleared a few cobwebs in her head. She gestured toward his ring with irritated exaggeration. "*And* you're a m-married man."

Ian's expression clouded for an instant, then his gaze darted to his hand. Piper rolled her eyes. *As if he'd forgotten he was wearing a wedding band.* She sighed, disappointed. "Look, I'm sure there are lots of women who don't mind the fact that you're supposed to be committed to another woman, but I'm not one of them."

He didn't speak, but simply stared at his ring. Suddenly, the day's events descended upon her: the worry of earning the bonus, the humiliating incident in the parking lot and an afternoon with her worst allergen for the sake of her job. On top of it all, now the medication was pulling at her limbs, weighing her down.

She blinked back hot tears of frustration. "How ironic that I meet you at the very time in my life when I'm trying to sort out the pros and cons of having a committed relationship." Piper tried to laugh. "Good night, Mr. Bentley. Go back to your motel room and call the woman who thinks you're being faithful." Piper stepped inside and closed the door with a solid thunk.

Ian stared at the door for a full minute before returning to his car in a daze. Inside lingered the smell of the greasy burgers and fries they'd shared mere moments before, amidst lighthearted banter. He couldn't remember enjoying a woman's company more—asking Piper for a kiss had seemed proper, and extracting the kiss had seemed…necessary.

He jerked his head around at the sound of someone rapping on the car window. Piper's spitting neighbor stood outside, still glaring. Setting his jaw, Ian buzzed down the window. "Yes?"

"Don't you be bothering Piper," the man warned.

What was his name—Len? ''I have no intention of bothering Piper,'' Ian assured him.

''It's a good thing, mister.'' Spit Man jerked a thumb into his own chest. ''Because that's *my* job.''

At a loss for words, Ian was glad to be distracted by the sight of two vehicles coming down the narrow road. He recognized the pharmacy guy driving Piper's van, and realized morosely that the rest of Ms. Shepherd's cavalry had arrived. He lifted his hand in an acquiescent wave to her neighbor, then turned over the engine, backed out and headed toward the motel.

Darkness had descended, making finding his way back a little tricky on the secondary roads lacking streetlights. Gritting his teeth, Ian whacked the steering wheel hard with his left hand. Too late, he remembered the ring. Waves of pain bounced through his hand and up his wrist. Ian cursed several times, each time louder than the last, until his voice reverberated inside the car.

Never before had he felt like such a colossal jerk. He'd told himself he wouldn't allow another woman to distract him from the decision he needed to make about Meredith, and instead, he'd kissed the first beauty who crossed his path—a woman with whom he also had to work, and who was apparently wrestling with a personal decision similar to his… Did she have a lover? Ian dragged his hand down his face. Of course a woman like Piper had a lover.

Tomorrow he would apologize to Piper, but tonight he would call the woman who thought he was being faithful.

# CHAPTER SIX

*When it comes to forgiving, be a lady. When it comes to forgetting, be an elephant.*

"NO MAN is worth all this," Nurse Browning said, surveying the rash on Piper's chest and arms. She shook her head, clucking. "Nice underwear, but if you don't lay off the chocolate, the hunky boss man won't want to get close enough to see it."

Piper smirked and rebuttoned her blouse over the lacy bra. "I came for medical care, not therapy," she said, reaching for her lab coat.

Janet shrugged. "Not much I can do about the rash. Just keep using the lotion and don't scratch—it's not very sexy."

"Enough already."

"Ah, come on, Piper, you can tell me." She leaned forward and lowered her voice to a conspiratorial whisper. "Has he made a pass at you yet?"

A night of staring at the ceiling, mulling over Ian's kiss, had left her psyche feeling more raw than her rash-ridden arms and chest. Piper leaned forward and lowered her voice to the same octave. "He's married, Janet, repeat after me—'married.'" Then she straightened and smiled. "Besides, I have a date tomorrow night."

Her friend's eyes widened. "With him?"

Piper's smile vanished. "No, not with him! Haven't you heard anything I just said?"

"Rich?"

She wondered if Janet suspected the truth about her assistant. "Uh, no."

"Who then?"

"Henry Walden."

Worry creased the woman's freckled face. "You'd better watch Henry—that man has more hands than Timex."

Piper scoffed. "You're trying to push me into the arms of a married man, but you're warning me about Henry?"

"At least that other fellow seems like a gentleman—Henry's a Casanova."

"Surely he won't try anything on the first date."

Looking sympathetic, Janet shook her head. "You'd better take a Bible with you."

Squinting, Piper angled her head at the red-haired woman. "What on earth are you talking about?"

"A Bible is the best defense a girl can have—just hold it between your knees all night."

"Since *you* are going to be struck by lightning," Piper declared, standing and reaching for her purse, "*I* am getting the heck out of here. Thanks for re-wrapping my ankle."

"Don't mention it. Say, are you working with what's-his-name this afternoon?"

Piper sighed. "You mean, Mr. Bentley?"

"Yeah."

Piper checked her watch, trying to maintain a calm exterior. "He's supposed to meet me in the lab in about an hour."

Janet leaned on a tall counter, resting her chin on her palm. "Well, since *you* don't want him, do you think you could manage to nick him with a paring knife? Just something superficial that might require a stitch or two?"

Piper wagged her finger in warning. "*You* need help." Laughing, she negotiated the short trip up-stairs to her office, forcing herself to focus on her work instead of the fact that she'd be with Ian all afternoon. She grabbed a pack of peanut-butter crackers from the vending machine for lunch—tast-ing sweets all morning had dulled her appetite. And the worst of it was that she hadn't yet hit a home run with any of the chocolate desserts she'd created. They'd all ended up down the disposal.

After propping up her twinging ankle, she made a couple of phone calls and caught up on some paperwork she'd been putting off. She had just gathered notes for her dreaded meeting when the phone rang. Half hoping the caller would be Ian canceling, she picked up the receiver.

"Piper Shepherd."

"Piper, dear, it's Gran."

She smiled into the phone. "Gran! What a nice surprise." When her grandmother did not immediately respond, she sat ramrod straight. "Is something wrong?"

"Not really. Actually, it's what I'd hoped for."

"What?"

"An offer on the house."

Piper swallowed and gripped the phone. "An offer? Th-that's great, Gran. Anyone I know?" If she couldn't have the house herself, perhaps the house would at least be bought by a nice family.

"The Realtor told me his name is Benjamin Warner."

"Warner? Is he from around here?"

"No, Boston."

Trying to force cheer into her voice, Piper said, "He must be a tourist."

"I don't think so."

Alert to the timbre of worry in her grandmother's voice, she asked, "Is there something you're not telling me?"

"The agent told me the man was especially interested in the zoning specifications where the house sits.''

''There *is* no zoning outside of Mudville city limits.''

''I know,'' her grandmother replied irritably. ''A person could build a funeral home in their backyard if they wanted to.''

''You think he plans to use the house commercially?''

Granny Falkner sighed. ''The Realtor told me from the beginning it would make an ideal bed-and-breakfast.''

Piper's heart sank. ''And you think that's what this Warner fellow is going to do?''

''It makes sense.''

''Has he offered the price you're asking?''

''Yes, but I'm not so sure I want to see my home turned into a hotel.''

''Do you have to give him an answer right away?''

''No, the offer is good for seven days.''

Which might give her time to secure that bonus and match the offer, Piper thought frantically. Of course, she'd be eating pork 'n beans into the foreseeable future, but she didn't care—she wanted her grandmother's house.

''Then take the next week and think about it,''

Piper urged. "Between now and then, someone else might make an offer that's more to your liking."

"I don't know," her grandmother fretted. "There aren't many folks around here who can afford to pay what this house is worth. And the out-of-towners who can afford it aren't exactly rushing to move to Mudville. Maybe I should lower the price to attract a nice young family around here."

"Gran," Piper chided. "This is your retirement we're talking about. You and Gramps invested a lot of money in building and maintaining that house. You have to get the best price possible."

"You're right, of course. I suppose I can't worry about what happens to the house once it's sold."

Piper pressed her lips together, then said, "A wise woman once told me that things don't always work out the way we plan, but somehow they always work out for the best."

Granny Falkner's soft laugh sounded over the line. "Sounds like good advice."

"The best. Don't worry, okay?"

Her grandmother sighed. "When did you get so grown-up?"

"I'll call you this evening. I love you." Piper hung up the phone slowly.

Rich came around the partition between their work areas holding a cup of instant soup and settled himself on the edge of her desk. "Love? Well, that was either your grandmother or the illustrious Mr. Bentley.''

Piper gasped, then shook her finger at her attractive co-worker. "That was Gran, you rat.''

He scooped noodles into his mouth and swallowed. "The man's got a thing for you, Piper.''

She smirked. "The man's got a wedding ring, Rich.''

He pursed his lips and nodded. "I noticed. Pity, too. The two of you would make a great couple.''

The memory of Ian's kiss, never far from her mind since she'd closed and locked the back door last night, washed over her anew. She glanced away, her cheeks burning with shame.

Rich leaned closer, narrowing his eyes. "What happened?''

Stapling a stack of reports, Piper kept her voice light. "I don't know what you're talking about.''

He smiled. "Then let me be more specific. What happened last night when he dropped you off at your place?''

She pulled back, indignant. "How the devil do you know about that?''

Rich abandoned his spoon and tipped the paper cup to his mouth to drain the broth, keeping her in suspense until he lowered the cup with a satisfied sigh. "It was on the blackboard at Alma's this morning.''

Panicked, Piper half rose out of her seat. "What?"

He laughed and chucked her under the chin. "I'm kidding. I was inside the burger joint last night having a romantic dinner with a bad paperback and I saw him drive around." Adopting a dubious expression, he added, "And I could have *sworn* that was you in the passenger seat."

Busted, she could only relent. "Okay, long story short, I accidentally took a painkiller and Gary wouldn't let me drive. I ran into Ian—er, Mr. Bentley, and he was kind enough to offer me a ride home."

"And I know how you can't resist kind men," Rich said dryly.

"He didn't even come inside," she added through clenched teeth.

"Glad to hear you practice safe sex." He winked at her and dodged her swatting hand, then sobered slightly. "Relax, Piper, I know you're much too moral to stoop to fooling around with a married man." Then he picked up her hand and sandwiched it between his in a rare display of affection. "But you're too good a catch to be languishing in a place like Mudville."

Squeezing his hand, she angled her head. "And I might say the same thing about you, Rich," she murmured, a gentle reminder of what he was running from.

He gave her a small sheepish smile, but the sound of a man clearing his throat interrupted them. Glancing toward the entrance, her heart jumped when she saw Ian walking slowly toward them, his gaze politely averted.

Rich released her hand and rose to his feet. Piper squirmed as Ian drew closer.

Dressed in navy suit slacks and a taupe-colored collarless dress shirt, he looked just as devastating as he had the day before, except for the faint circles under his bloodshot eyes. Ian Bentley had not slept so well on the mattress he'd been praising yesterday—a guilty conscience? A black leather briefcase hung from his beringed left hand.

Piper sat up and squared her shoulders. "Good afternoon, Mr. Bentley." Disappointment resounded in her chest that she could still be so affected by him after knowing about his deceptive nature.

"Ms. Shepherd," he responded lightly, his eyes unreadable. "Mr. Enderling." The men shook hands, then Rich excused himself with one last meaningful look at Piper.

Ian set his briefcase on her desk, glanced around the open office area, then asked, "Is there somewhere we can talk?"

Piper stood abruptly and gathered her notes for the afternoon session. "About the project? Of course." She swept her arm in the direction of the lab. "Shall we?"

For an instant, he hesitated, then inclined his head and walked beside her. He remained silent, as did she, although she could hear her own shallow breathing. They entered the lab, and as she made her way to a computer workstation, Piper reviewed her plan mentally: stay focused on the project and steer clear of discussing their personal encounter.

"About last night—" he began.

"Yes," she cut in casually, turning a friendly smile his way, "I didn't thank you for dinner and the ride home."

Ian set his briefcase on the counter with slow, deliberate movements. "You're welcome," he said evenly. "Piper—"

The door to the lab swung open, admitting Rich. "Sorry, Piper, but this is the fax you were waiting for."

Grateful for the timely interruption, she scanned the paper he handed her, refusing to acknowledge his knowing expression. "Thanks, Rich," she said in dismissal, but he stood rooted until she glanced up again. His left eyebrow quirked a fraction. "Thank you, Rich," she repeatedly pointedly. Her assistant nodded curtly, shot a look toward Ian, then left.

With her body humming in awareness of Ian's proximity, Piper studied the sheet. "Good news— marketing secured co-op offers from Peabody's peanut butter, and from both Chico's and Sandal's chocolate, among others. We can reduce your ingredient cost, plus benefit from the impact of the brand name if we tag it on your new dessert."

"Nice work," he admitted, then took the sheet from her and laid it on the counter. When he glanced back, Piper's pulse kicked up. He seemed determined to discuss their indiscretion.

His gray eyes were troubled. "Piper, we need to talk about last night."

Panicked, she rubbed her hands over her arms and walked around the other side of the counter to gain an emotionally safe distance. After a deep breath, she turned back to face him. "There's nothing to discuss, Ian."

He held up his hands. "Just hear me out."

At his obvious irritation, her temper flared. She leaned forward, splaying her hands on the counter. She pasted a pleasant expression on her face, but injected a hard edge into her voice. "Mr. Bentley, I really don't care to listen to how your wife doesn't understand you—"

"I'm not married."

"—or that you have an open relationship...." She stopped and squinted. "What did you say?"

"I'm not married."

A wave of terror washed over her. Not only had she made a fool of herself yet again, not to mention insulting the character of their largest client, but she realized with alarming clarity that she'd considered his married status insurance against yielding to her physical attraction to him.

She realized he was waiting for her reaction, and she felt frozen in place. Commanding her mouth to move, she tested words on her tongue. "Y-you're not m-married?"

A glint of amusement flashed in his eyes, but he didn't smile. "No, I'm not."

Her gaze involuntarily flew to the ring on his left hand. She straightened and crossed her arms self-consciously, yearning to scratch her chest and neck and back. "Th-then why didn't you say something last night?" To what end, she thought, and shuddered at the possibilities.

His chest expanded as he inhaled deeply, and Piper realized there was more to the story.

All morning Ian had steeled himself against Piper's allure, telling himself he could clarify the situation and apologize without digging himself deeper into a pit of lust. But he hadn't realized how much he'd been looking forward to their meeting until he'd seen her sitting at her desk. Absurd jealously had bolted through him at the sight of her assistant holding her hand so intimately. At least now he knew which man Piper had been referring to when she'd said she was also contemplating a committed relationship.

"But I *am* involved with someone," he said finally. She blinked, but her expression remained unreadable. Ian cleared his throat and nodded to the ring on his left hand. "She, um, proposed the day before I left Chicago, and I told her I'd let her know when I return." When she offered no response, he pursed his lips, then continued, "So you were right—no matter how attracted I am to you, I had no business kissing you last night."

He hesitated, foolishly half hoping she would assure him she too felt the attraction rebounding between them and fully understood his reaction. She didn't, forcing him to proceed. "I apologize for placing you in a compromising situation. If you would prefer I work with another scientist on this project, I understand."

Her eyes widened slightly. "Um, no, I'm committed to seeing this project through until the end."

He nodded, respecting her dedication. "I could return to Chicago and send a representative in a couple of weeks—"

"No," she cut in rather brusquely. "I mean…

I've already prepared a few samples, and I was hoping we could wrap this up within a couple of days.''

Ian studied her for a few seconds, aware of her discomfort, wishing he could put her at ease, wishing he could convincingly reassure her and himself that he would not be thinking about their solitary kiss every moment he was with her. ''I wouldn't want all your work this morning to be for nothing.'' He attempted a smile. ''And besides, I'm hungry.''

At last she smiled, a welcome sight, though a mere shadow of the spectacular eye-lighting grins he had become accustomed to seeing. His heart lifted a notch. ''Am I forgiven?''

She seemed surprised, and her smile slipped. ''On hindsight, what happened hardly seems like a sin.''

''It's important to know I haven't offended you.''

She blushed and raked her hand lightly over her chest. ''In that case, yes, all is forgiven.''

Enormously relieved, yet bothered that her opinion had become so important to him in such a short time, Ian patted the counter for emphasis. ''Good.''

Piper nodded somewhat stiffly toward the white table. ''Well then, let's get down to business, shall we?''

Ian made his way toward the table and tried not to watch Piper as she walked, still limping slightly, to a commercial-size refrigerator. She'd traded her jeans, T-shirt and sneakers for loose black slacks, a light-colored blouse peeking through her knee-length blue lab coat and sensible flats. With her dark hair tucked behind small ears, her cheekbones and those piercing ice-blue eyes were even more prominent. She resembled a neat little package just begging to be unwrapped. Ian swallowed and busied himself removing notes from his briefcase.

She withdrew a covered tray and carried it to the table, but she scrupulously avoided making eye contact with him. A sense of loss stabbed him, for which he sternly chastised himself. Undoubtedly, most of the attraction he felt for Piper was triggered by his panic over Meredith's sudden proposal.

''I hope to have more chocolate recipes tomorrow,'' she said as she lifted the cover. Beneath sat an assortment of four desserts on individual plates. She named each one as she pointed. ''Lemon meringue mousse, cherry and cream cheese parfait, cinnamon layer cake with chocolate icing and caramel-pecan clusters in phyllo pastry.''

His mouth was already watering, and he dearly hoped it was due to the food. ''I'm impressed.''

''I'm glad,'' she said cheerfully. After arranging several forks and spoons next to the tray, she handed him a napkin. He took the soft cloth, dismayed at the electric charge when their fingers brushed. She must have felt it, too, because she immediately dropped her hand and her gaze, then turned toward a freezer. "I'll get a sorbet to cleanse your palate between dishes."

Glancing between the colorful concoctions, each different, but beautifully presented, Ian sighed. "I've never liked having to choose," he said, regretting the words as soon as they left his mouth.

With her back to him, it was difficult to discern if she'd noticed the Freudian slip. She returned to the table bearing a clear glass bowl of garnished lime sorbet and a tight smile. "That's life," she said lightly.

She'd noticed, all right. He squirmed and felt a flush climb his cheeks.

She situated the sorbet near him, then took the seat farthest away, poised with a pen to make notes as they moved through each dish. There was something decidedly provocative about eating a beautiful dessert while looking at a beautiful woman, Ian decided.

He chose the lemon-meringue mousse first and dipped in the end of a spoon, scooping up a dollop the size of a cotton ball. Somewhat self-consciously, he lifted the spoon and slowly placed the yellow puddinglike dessert into his mouth. His taste buds tingled as soon as the cool, creamy tang hit his tongue. Holding the creation against the roof of his mouth, he savored the light, tart flavor.

With a start, he realized that Piper, sitting at the other end of the table, held her gaze riveted to his mouth. Her eyes were soft around the edges, and she moved her empty mouth in synchronization with his. He chewed, she chewed. He pursed his lips, she pursed hers. He swallowed, her throat constricted. His body reacted, and he imagined hers responding, too.

"Very nice," he croaked, shifting in his seat.

Piper started, then slid a fact sheet across the table. "Ingredient measurements, costs and nutrition breakdown per serving," she explained.

Ian picked up his pen and made notes of his own at the bottom of the sheet. *Soft, creamy and sensual.*

The refreshing sorbet chilled his tongue and, thankfully, his expanding desire. With his heart pounding in relief, he picked up another spoon and turned to the parfait. He knew he was doomed, however, when he withdrew the utensil only to find a round, red cherry dangling from the end.

His gaze darted to Piper, who seemed mesmerized. She licked her lips slowly, then said, "Of course, the cherries are local, er, *grown* locally, that is."

"Of course," he murmured. Figuring it was best to get it over with, he plunged the spoonful into his mouth. This time, instead of torturing himself with a slow contemplation, he kept his eyes off Piper and nearly swallowed the portion whole. Naturally, the cherry lodged in the back of his throat. He swallowed painfully several times, lapsing into a coughing fit as a finale. She sprang up and retrieved a glass of water, which he gratefully accepted.

At the bottom of the sheet she passed him, he wrote *should be savored, not rushed.*

He swirled the sorbet around in his mouth and used the napkin to wipe the perspiration from his forehead.

"Ah, chocolate," he said, slicing a fork into the pinkish two-layer cinnamon cake dripping with dark icing. He shoved in a mouthful and crushed together the rich icing and surprisingly spicy cake. Piper seemed to be captivated by the notes in front of her. He swallowed and reached for the fact sheet.

She glanced up and met him halfway, staring at him with an odd expression in her eyes. When her rosy tongue appeared and made a leisurely trip around her lips, he forgot what he'd intended to write. Stone-still, he watched as her tongue reappeared and reached new lengths in its second trip around her bow-shaped mouth. This time he doubted the cold taste of the sorbet would be efficient to douse his burgeoning erection. She leaned forward and pointed to a spot above the corner of her mouth. Then he realized she was trying to tell him he had something on his face. Chocolate icing, no doubt.

He wiped his mouth with the napkin, but she shook her head. He wiped higher, then lower, but she shook her head and giggled.

"I'll get it," she offered. She stood and took his napkin, then dabbed at the corner of his mouth. Ian sat perfectly immobile, catching a whiff of something medicinal as she leaned close to him. Small and well-shaped, her hands were free of jewelry. He gulped a deep breath and exhaled slowly. The desire to pull her down into his lap was overwhelming. Almost involuntarily, he reached up and encircled her wrist.

She went still, pulling back a millimeter, her breath suddenly ragged. In her wide eyes, he glimpsed the fire lurking just beneath the surface. "You'd better let me," he declared. Ian released his grip and took the napkin from her shaking hand.

"Okay," she whispered, then straightened. "More water?"

"The colder the better."

"I think I'll join you."

While she prepared the much-needed neutralizer, Ian found the fact sheet and wrote *sweet on the outside, fiery on the inside*.

Piper set down a glass of water next to him and

hurried back to her own seat so quickly a few drops sloshed over the edge.

For the phyllo-pastry creation, Ian abandoned utensils, which seemed like a good idea until he bit down and the filling oozed over his fingers. The buttery paper-thin pastry dissolved against his tongue, allowing the rich, gooey caramel to flood his taste buds. He groaned his pleasure and rolled his eyes heavenward. Another bite finished off the pastry, and Ian's fingers were halfway to his mouth before he remembered he had an audience. He stopped, midmotion, and glanced up guiltily.

Piper sat with her dark eyebrows raised, an amused smile on her face. "I take it the caramel pastry is your favorite?"

"Um, yeah."

She laughed into her hand, her shoulders shaking.

Ian laughed, too, but mostly out of sheer pleasure at seeing her happy again. He tried to clean his sticky hands with the napkin, but gave up and walked over to one of the three utility sinks to wash. He walked back to the table, drying his hands on a paper towel.

Still grinning, she slid the fact sheet in front of where he stopped to lean. "Unfortunately, it's by far the most expensive choice."

He scanned the sheet. "Ouch."

"I know—we could try to get co-op dollars from

Conner's caramels, but even though they own the market, I personally doubt the brand name is strong enough for you to benefit.''

"Disappointing, but true, I'm afraid," Ian agreed. Across the bottom, he scribbled *desirable, but out of reach.*

"I'll have more samples for you tomorrow morning," she promised. "Lots of chocolate." She scratched lightly along the neckline of her blouse. "Then you can make your selection."

"Allergies still bothering you?" he asked.

She nodded and stood, rolling her shoulders.

"I happen to be a great back-scratcher," he offered.

"I'll have to take your word for it," she said with a wry smile. "We're finished here, if you have something else to do."

Patting his stomach, he laughed. "I'd like to work off a few of the calories I just consumed." Another faux pas in light of the sexually charged atmosphere, he realized a syllable too late. At her "now, now" expression, he sighed. "I think I'd better go before I say something I'll *really* regret."

He shuffled the fact sheets, reviewing each one as he placed them in his briefcase. *Soft, creamy and sensual…should be savored, not rushed…sweet on the outside, fiery on the inside…desirable, but out of reach.* It didn't take a psychology degree to see where his mind had been during the sampling session. Shaking his head, he glanced up to find Piper watching him, her mouth set in a straight line, her eyes rueful. Beautiful, funny, sexy. And some other man held her affection. The thought made his gut clench.

"Tell me, Piper," he said slowly, "is your assistant, Mr. Enderling, from Mudville?"

She shook her head. "No, Ohio."

"Long way from home," he observed.

"Rich and I met in college at MSU."

"Ah," he murmured, pressing down the brass tabs on his briefcase. "And may I ask who followed whom to Mudville?"

She shrugged and began clearing the table. "Edmund offered me the job and said I could hire my own assistant. Rich and I had stayed in touch, and when I mentioned the job to him, he jumped at it."

Jumped at the chance to be with Piper, Ian thought. Well, he couldn't argue with the man's taste. And from what he'd seen of the local offering of eligible bachelors, Piper had made a wise move in bringing her companion to town. "There, um, don't seem to be a lot of men in town like Mr. Enderling," he offered, thinking the mild compliment was the least he owed her after last night.

At the sound of the tray clattering against the table, he glanced up to find her eyes blazing. "Mr.

Bentley,'' she said evenly, ''I certainly don't intend to discuss Rich Enderling with you of all people.''

He'd hit a nerve. Apparently their romance was on the rocks, which explained her participation in the kiss he'd initiated last night.

Piper stalked toward the door, then turned back and threw him a smirk. ''By the way, Mr. Bentley, I do hope you sleep better tonight.''

Ian suspected she might have slammed the door had it not been hydraulic. After replaying his idiotic words in his mind, he decided his briefcase would suffice, and banged it shut with both hands.

## CHAPTER SEVEN

*Forget about his stomach—jealousy is the quickest way to a man's heart.*

"I'M JUST NOT SURE what to do." Granny Falkner smiled sadly.

"You still have time to think about the offer," Piper assured her, fighting to keep the disappointment out of her voice. She ran a dust mop along the baseboard of "her" room, the guest room where she'd slept since childhood. The white iron bed sat naked, devoid of sheets, the mattress piled high with boxes of linens and whatnot.

"Maybe I'll be less sentimental after I'm tucked away at Greenbay Ridge."

"Probably," Piper agreed.

"I asked the real-estate agent to contact this Mr. Warner and find out exactly what he has in mind, although once he buys the house I suppose he can do anything he chooses with it, no matter what he tells me."

"Perhaps we're jumping to conclusions, Gran. Maybe the man is rich and simply wants a country getaway."

"Perhaps." Suddenly her grandmother stopped and leaned on her broom. "Addy Purdue told me you were in the pharmacy last night talking to a strange man."

Piper tossed a wry smile over her shoulder. "Are you sure she wasn't referring to her son Gary?"

Gran laughed. "I don't think so. Fess up."

Determined to keep her mixed emotions about Ian a safely guarded secret, she forced a casual note into her voice. "There's nothing to confess—his name is Ian Bentley. He's from Chicago and he's an important customer. I'm trying to come up with a new dessert for a line of coffeehouses he owns."

"Oooh." Her grandmother's voice dripped with suggestion. "Have you known him long?"

Piper hid her warm cheeks by reaching for an elusive cobweb. "We nearly rammed each other in the parking lot yesterday morning, then I made a complete fool out of myself by spraining my ankle. He carried me into the building—"

"*Carried* you?"

She nodded, her stomach lurching at the memory. "Only then did I discover he was the infamous restaurateur I was supposed to wow with an irresistible dessert."

"Oh my." Gran's shoulders shook with mirth, and she hid her mouth behind her hand. "Forgive me, my dear. And have you been able to impress him with your banana-cream trifle?"

"He's allergic to bananas."

"Oh."

"But he *loves* chocolate."

"So that explains why you've been scratching all evening."

"Except he's difficult to please—I haven't been able to come up with a winner yet."

Her grandmother's blue eyes twinkled. "You will."

Piper glanced around the empty, beloved room, keeping her deeper worries to herself. "I hope so."

"So it was pure chance that you ran into him at the pharmacy?"

Piper stretched to run the mop over the top of a window frame. "I was buying allergy medicine, he was buying toothpaste. Mr. Purdue gave me a pain-killer for my ankle, but Gary failed to tell me until I'd taken it that I shouldn't drive."

"And let me guess—Gary offered you a ride home?"

"Yep."

Gran pursed her lips. "That boy might be smarter than I thought."

Piper laughed. "Well, at any rate, since Gary

wasn't quite ready to leave, Mr. Bentley offered to drop me off.''

''And is this Mr. Bentley single?''

Piper took a deep breath. ''Sort of.''

Her grandmother's pale eyebrows rose. ''Separated?''

''No. He's considering a marriage proposal.''

''Oh. Well, this is the nineties, after all.'' Granny Falkner cocked her head to one side. ''It sounds like the two of you are rather well acquainted if he's discussing his love life.''

The dust mop slipped from her hands and clattered to the floor. ''It just came up in conversation.''

''Before or after he made a pass at you?''

Piper jerked her head up and laughed nervously. ''Gran, I really don't think—''

''Piper.''

She sighed and bent to retrieve the mop. ''Okay...after.''

''And are you involved with him?''

''No.''

''But you'd like to be?''

Piper hesitated too long to fool her grandmother. Suddenly exhausted, she sat heavily on the floor and sagged against the wall. Tears sprang to her eyes. ''I don't know,'' she whispered.

''Hey, hey,'' her grandmother chided, joining her

on the floor. "I've never seen you shed tears over any man, much less a man you just met."

"That's just it, Gran," she mumbled miserably. "We're attracted to each other, I think, but he's completely wrong for me—even if he wasn't almost engaged. He's, he's too…charming and sexy and arrogant."

"Henry Walden is arrogant, too."

Piper frowned, lolling her head to the side. "Addy Purdue caught you up on all the gossip, didn't she?"

The other woman nodded. "And that Walden man doesn't even have anything to back up his arrogance."

"Henry's not so bad."

"Piper, you shouldn't settle for 'not so bad.'"

"At least Henry lives in Mudville."

Her grandmother propped up her chin with her palm. "I've heard Chicago is nice."

"Mudville is my home. I want to be near you, Gran."

Gran slipped an arm around her shoulders. "I'm glad you want to be close to me, dear, but you have to think about your future."

Piper scoffed. "I am, but my future is *not* with Ian Bentley."

"Never say never."

"He's getting married, Gran."

"He doesn't love the woman, Piper. He just hasn't admitted it to himself yet."

"What makes you so sure?"

"Because if two people are really in love, they can't contemplate a future without each other. He's stalling."

Piper refused to be mollified. "He's still all wrong for me."

"If that's so," her grandmother said, reaching forward to wipe her thumb over Piper's cheek, "then why the tears?"

Her eyes welled again, but she didn't want to burden her grandmother with all the muddled thoughts in her head. Things were not turning out the way she'd planned. She'd embarked on a man-hunt to marry a nice country fellow. She'd live in her grandmother's house, raise two well-adjusted children and eventually retire from Blythe Industries. It was a sensible plan, solid, dependable, safe—all the things she'd sworn her life would be someday.

"I'll make you a deal," her grandmother offered, squeezing her shoulders. "I won't worry if you won't worry."

Piper sniffed mightily and faked a smile. "Deal."

"Good. Now, let's get these boxes out to your van. I've got three days to get everything in order."

"What time will the movers be here on Saturday?"

"Around noon."

"I'll be here."

Her grandmother gave her a kiss on the temple. "Maybe by then some of our problems will be solved."

Piper smiled for the other woman's sake. For herself, she'd settle for things not getting any worse.

Later, as Piper pulled out of her grandmother's driveway in her loaded-down van, she adjusted the side mirror and glanced at the house that symbolized everything good in her life. It wasn't lost to her yet, but she needed that bonus in her red, itchy little hands.

After Ian had left the office, she'd spent the rest of the day experimenting with chocolate, drafting Rich to be her taster when she began to feel worse. And despite her effort, she still wasn't satisfied. Her creative juices had dried up—what hadn't been done with chocolate?

"Not your best," Rich had agreed, but helped her narrow down the selection to three choices: cocoa raspberry mousse, transparent chocolate tart and an uninspired chocolate cake.

A seemingly all-over itch shivered across her skin and she scratched as hard as she dared across her chest, stomach and as much of her back as she could reach while wearing a seat belt. She hoped she'd at least be back to normal before her date tomorrow night, but since she didn't plan on allowing Henry to examine her torso, she wasn't overly concerned. If and when she did decide to become intimate with anybody, Ian Bentley and her rash would be long gone.

With that disquieting thought, she channeled her concentration toward coming up with a dessert Ian Bentley couldn't resist. Early dusk had begun to settle when Piper arrived at her rented house. The phone was ringing insistently as she reached the back door. She dropped a small box of kitchen supplies onto the counter and grabbed the phone.

"Hello?"

"Piper, I need your measurements," Justine declared in her typical, no small-talk intro.

"Right now?"

"Yes, right now. My seamstress is on the other line, holding for them."

Piper rolled her eyes. "Can you give me a minute to find a tape measure?"

"Hurry, would you? All this long distance is costing me a fortune."

"And the wedding isn't," Piper muttered to herself as she laid the old handset on the counter.

She trotted to the hall closet and grabbed a tape measure from her dust-covered sewing basket, then hurried back to snatch up the phone. With a swipe at the wall beside the back door, she flipped on the tiny kitchen light. "Are you ready?" she asked, smoothing out the wrinkled tape.

"Yeah, I'm ready already."

Piper twisted and wrapped the tape around her back until it met over her breasts on top of her thin tank. Since she wasn't wearing a bra, it would be close enough, she decided. "Thirty-four."

After yanking up her shirt, she lowered the tape to her calamine lotion-covered waist. "Twenty-six."

"That's disgusting," Justine declared.

Fumbling, she unbuttoned her faded cutoffs and wiggled them down to her knees, holding the phone in the crook of her neck. With a lot of twisting and arching, she moved the tape lower over her skimpy cotton panties. "Thirty-five."

"I hate you," Justine insisted.

"Will that be all?" Piper asked, dropping the tape and tugging at her shorts.

"Just a reminder that you'll have to come early the day of the rehearsal dinner for a last-minute fitting."

"No problem. Did the salmon thing work out?"

"Yeah, the bridesmaids' gowns are adorable—yards and yards of fabric, and matching hair bows.

"Wow, no kidding—hair bows." Piper picked

up a steak knife and pretended to plunge it into her heart. What was it about weddings that sent otherwise tasteful women back to their childhood costume fantasies?

"Well, I have to run. Oh, by the way, have you met your hero yet?"

Juggling the phone, Piper dropped the knife, turned to refasten her shorts and froze. Ian Bentley stood at her front screen door in the fading daylight, holding a box he'd taken from her van. His gray eyes were riveted on her, his lips parted. Instantly she knew he had witnessed her entire performance, perfectly outlined by the kitchen light. The blood drained from her face so quickly, she felt faint.

"Goodbye, Justine, I have to kill myself." Piper slammed down the phone and briefly reconsidered the effectiveness of the steak knife. "Oh God, oh God," she mumbled, wrestling with the button at her navel. She gave up and simply stretched her pink tank down as far as the fabric would allow. After a few deep breaths, she lifted her gaze, praying he'd disappeared. He hadn't.

Squaring her shoulders, Piper pasted a smile on her face and walked to the front door. "Hello," she said through the screen, her tone even, as if nothing had happened.

Ian stared at her and swallowed painfully, unable to erase the image of her standing half-naked in the light at the far end of the house. Since the box was concealing a raging erection, he held on to it as if it were a lifeline. "I can see why your neighbor is always hanging around," he ventured with a small laugh.

"Did you want something, Ian?" she asked.

With sudden clarity, he decided that yes, he did want something—her. He averted his gaze to the box in his hands. "I was driving by and saw your van. It looked like you could use a hand."

She crossed her arms. "Driving by?"

"You're not going to make this easy, are you?"

"You're used to having things come to you easily, aren't you, Mr. Bentley?"

"Not always, but perhaps lately," he admitted honestly. "I didn't want to wait until tomorrow to apologize. My comment this afternoon about Mr. Enderling was out of line. You're right—it's none of my business."

She lifted a corner of her mouth and leaned against the door frame. "Finally we agree on something."

"If you'd rather I not come in, I can unload the boxes and set them on your porch," he offered, almost hoping she would keep the door between them, since he was precariously close to ripping through the flimsy screen and crushing her against him.

"No," she said, unfolding her arms slowly and reaching for the door latch. "Actually, I would appreciate you bringing them inside. I have a space cleared for the boxes in the spare bedroom."

He stepped back as she pushed open the door and adjusted the spring to hold it wide. Sweat dripped between his shoulder blades as he shifted the weight of the box and stepped inside. He followed her through the small house that reminded him of one he'd lived in as a boy—the same house his parents had mortgaged to give him his start more than fifteen years ago.

Decorated in refreshing blues and white, her tiny living room looked cool and inviting. Two striped couches sat in an L shape, a pale floral rug on the honey-colored wooden floor. Bright botanical prints in simple frames adorned the unpapered walls. A light-hued curio cabinet sat against the opposite wall, housing an extensive collection of salt-and-pepper shakers. And it seemed she was quite the movie buff, considering the titles stacked up on a bookcase. In the corner, a quiet fan worked furiously, circulating air in a house obviously devoid of an air conditioner.

Ian picked his way across the room carefully, then turned down a hallway not much wider than his shoulders. She walked past a bedroom bursting with sun-yellow linens, which he guessed was hers, and led him into a nearly empty bedroom in the corner of the house.

"Anywhere against the wall would be fine," she said, pointing to three other boxes sitting beneath a green-curtained window.

He lowered the box to the floor carefully, then stood and removed a handkerchief from his pocket to wipe his neck. "If you don't mind me asking," he said as they walked to the front of the house, "what is all this stuff?"

"It belongs to my grandmother." She smiled and accompanied him to the van. "She's cleaning out her closets and giving me all the things she can't bear to throw away."

He stood back while she rooted through the remaining boxes, trying to discern the contents before dragging them inside. "Gramps carved these," she said, holding up a pair of sleek wooden candlesticks. "And here's his favorite bank!" Her eyes shone as she caressed the side of a miniature Model-T. "He used to keep only wheat pennies inside." She shook it, grinning wide at the *chink, chink* of coins sliding around.

Ian felt a pang of longing for his own family as he watched her. He'd always been close to his parents while he was at home, but once he moved out on his own, their time together had dwindled more and more as his company had grown larger and larger. He hadn't seen them in months. They would love Piper, he thought. Suddenly, he stopped and shook the stray notion from his head. Meredith knew him, she understood him, she loved him. He hardly knew the slip of a woman before him.

Yet she *was* engaging, he had to admit. He bit back a groan as she leaned over a box, pulling the cutoff shorts high and tight across her tanned thighs.

They made three more trips, she carrying the lighter boxes, he carrying the heavier ones—she limping slightly due to her ankle, he limping slightly due to an almost constant state of arousal he managed to keep hidden.

Most of the cartons went to the bedroom, but the last one she directed him to deposit in the kitchen, a cracker-box room neatly decorated with framed, hand-written recipes. Most of the floor space was taken up with a beautifully scarred rectangular butcher-block table at least six inches thick, with a surface almost as large as a twin bed. ''Nice,'' he said, stroking the surface.

''Thanks,'' she said, opening the refrigerator door and peering inside. ''Old man Richardson gave me the table when he closed his meat shop a while back. I must have sanded a half inch off the surface to get down to the good wood again. Iced tea?''

He nodded, wiping his neck and forehead again. "It's hot," he said unnecessarily. He could no longer turn the ring on his finger—his skin had expanded with the humidity. If he didn't marry Meredith, he supposed he'd have to get the thing cut off. Ian stopped—the thought had popped into his head unbidden.

Piper closed the refrigerator and laughed. "It's summer, and you're in Mississippi—it's supposed to be hot." Nodding toward the bulky table, she said, "Have a seat and I'll pour."

Ian pulled out the chair at the short end of the table and lowered himself gingerly. He had a tight feeling in his chest that indicated something was going to happen between them, and a tight feeling in his pants that told him whatever it was, he welcomed it.

Piper set a sweating glass of amber-colored liquid in front of him. "Sugar?"

He shook his head and lifted the glass to his mouth, trying not to stare at the wet spots on her thin shirt where she'd held the cold pitcher of tea against her. After a long drink, he passed a hand over his face and settled back in the chair.

Still standing, Piper leaned over and with a little grunt lifted the window to his left. Warmish air floated in, stirring the sheer white curtains. She dropped into the remaining seat on the long side of the table, close enough for their knees to brush. The movement made her breasts jiggle and made him clamp his hands around the cool glass.

She tucked her sweat-dampened hair behind her ears, and Ian's breath caught in his throat at her glistening beauty. After adding a packet of artificial sweetener to her tea, she stirred it with her finger, then casually licked off the liquid. Lifting the glass to her mouth, she drank as deeply as he had. He watched, mesmerized, as the slim column of her throat constricted.

"Whew." She set down her glass and lifted a paper towel to her neck. "Thank you. It would have taken me all evening to unload the van."

His fingers were numb from squeezing his glass. "Glad to be of service. You have a nice place here."

"It's okay," she conceded. "But I'd like to have a place of my own one of these days. Do you live alo—I mean, do you live in an apartment?"

He nodded. "I live alone and I live in an apartment."

"You probably travel a great deal."

He thought about his family. "Probably more than I should." He swallowed another mouthful of cold tea, then cleared his throat. "Um, Piper."

"Yeah?"

Despite his best efforts, a smile erupted. "What exactly were you doing when I arrived?"

She sank white teeth into her lower lip and blushed furiously. "Taking my measurements. I'm going to be in a friend's wedding in August."

He laughed loudly, shifting his legs. Their knees bumped again. "I've been in a few weddings myself. Ever been the bride?"

Shaking her head, she said, "Always a bridesmaid. And after being in some of the biggest productions east of Las Vegas, my ideal wedding would be to leave town quietly then come back married." She smiled and wiped sweat from her glass in little up-and-down motions. "You? Ever been married, I mean?"

"No." His heart beat erratically and he took a shaky breath. "Not yet."

She nodded. "It's a big decision."

He nodded. "Huge."

"Life-altering," she added, still nodding.

"Till death do us part," he agreed, still nodding.

"I'm sure she's a nice lady."

No reason to stop nodding, he decided. "She is."

"Beautiful?"

"Yes."

She sipped her tea again. "Have you known her long?"

"Six years now, I think."

"Oh, that's good," she said, rattling her glass to settle the ice. "Because you really need to know someone before you, um, you know—"

"Do something that will change the course of your life?"

"Exactly," she said, then pointed a finger and added. "And the other person's life, too."

He nodded. "Right. One impetuous decision could trigger a series of disasters."

"I couldn't agree more."

"For instance, if I were to kiss you again right now," he said, thinking how much he liked this nodding thing.

Her nodding slowed, but didn't stop. "Good example—yes, that could very well trigger a series of disasters."

Before he could talk himself out of it, he leaned forward and curled his fingers around the back of her hot, slender neck. The wet ends of her hair tickled his palm as he slowly pulled her forward. Her darkly fringed ice-blue eyes were wide with surprise and uncertainty, and he wondered if his own eyes reflected the same emotions. Desire gripped him and lashed itself around his body like steel bands. Her breath whooshed out, cool and sweet, and he inhaled her spent air a split second before capturing her wet mouth with his.

He explored the recesses of her mouth with his

tongue, taking everything and wanting more. She moved her mouth over his with no trace of timidity, conquering in her own right, draining him. Ian felt himself falling into her, past the point of no return. Nothing could stop the momentum of their need for each other.

The peal of the phone rent the air, and Piper stiffened. Ian knew he'd lost her, but urged her on with his mouth. But she turned her head, breaking their kiss, and covered her mouth with a shaking hand. On the third ring, she jumped up and lifted the phone from its cradle, turning her back to him. "H-hello?"

Unwilling to let her go, Ian stood on unsure knees and strode over to stand directly behind her. When she didn't acknowledge him, he touched the back of his fingers to the sensitive area of her neck she unwittingly exposed by shoving back her wet hair. But instead of melting into him, she froze, then stepped away from him.

"Oh, hello, Henry. I'm doing fine." Apparently she thought it would be safer to keep her eye on him, because she suddenly pivoted to face him and leaned her hips against the counter. At least she appeared to be as shaken as he was—she barely made eye contact.

But who the hell was Henry?

"Yeah, it's hot," she agreed breathlessly.

"Hmm? Out of breath? Oh, I've been—" she flicked her gaze over him "—exercising."

Ian set his jaw, and reached for her again. But she held up her hand to stop him.

"Seven o'clock tomorrow night," she said to Henry, a bit too cheerfully for Ian's liking. "I'll be ready. Goodbye." She hung up the phone, but maintained her position against the counter, her gaze on her shoes.

"I take it that wasn't Rich," he said quietly.

An irritated noise emerged from her throat and she glanced up. "That's right." Piper straightened. "Just someone I have a date with tomorrow night, that's all."

She was trying to make her boyfriend jealous. Ian looked away and jammed his hand through his hair. "I guess I'd better be going."

"I guess so."

"Are we still on for tomorrow morning?"

For an instant, she looked remorseful. "Yes. I hope you don't let this, this...*incident* cloud your business judgment—Blythe is still the best company to fill your contract."

Annoyed at her insinuation that he would let personal issues interfere with doing his job, he only hoped she would deliver something wonderful enough to make his choice an easy one.

# CHAPTER EIGHT

*During the first date, score your suitor on a scale from one to one hundred. To predict his husbandly behavior, divide by two.*

FROM HER SEAT at the end of the lab table, Piper fidgeted, watching the chances of getting her bonus soon dwindle as Ian moved from the cocoa-raspberry mousse to the transparent chocolate tart with no comment. He shook his dark head almost indiscernibly while scribbling notes on the bottom of each fact sheet.

With the previous night's events hanging between them, their interaction had been limited to nods and monosyllabic words. A stone of worry and regret lay in her stomach. Although the chocolate desserts probably weren't going to win him over, she felt sure the flirtation that she'd encouraged, then stopped abruptly, hadn't exactly helped her cause.

His eyes did light up at the sight of the simple

chocolate layer cake, though. "Chocolate cake—my all-time favorite," he murmured, probably because the silence was making him uncomfortable. With her fingers crossed under the table, she watched his face as he chewed, then swallowed.

"It's very good," he pronounced, nodding and making notes. Then he lay down his pen and pushed the tray aside.

"But?" she prompted, already knowing the verdict.

"But," he repeated slowly, "I'm looking for a recipe that strikes a balance between uniqueness and price point, and the white chocolate mousse I sampled at the plant in Illinois seems to come the closest to those requirements."

Piper released a breath she hadn't realized she'd been holding. She tried very hard to concentrate on his words, but disappointment mixed with images from last night tumbled over and over in her head. And it seemed incongruous that mere conversation flowed from the mouth which last night had induced such an amazing physical reaction within her. If Henry hadn't called, they would have probably been late for their own meeting this morning.

He picked up his pen, uncapped it, recapped it, then laid it back down. "Piper, look, I know this is an awkward situation, and I want to prove to you and to myself that I'm being as fair as possible.

Take a few days, take a month if you need it. Give me a moderately priced premium chocolate cake, have marketing slap a catchy name on it, and you have my word that Blythe will get my business.''

Her ears strained, listening for any little inflection that would indicate he was playing games. As always, he sounded calm, collected, in control. It was obvious that their encounter had not affected him as much as it had affected her. She felt like a country bumpkin, naive and ignorant of the ways of the world, of the ways of worldly men.

''Your offer seems more than fair,'' she agreed, then steepled her hands and chose her words carefully. ''But we could have saved a lot of time if you had simply told me you wanted chocolate cake.''

He smiled tightly. ''Well, I like to try new things, but I guess when it comes down to it—''

''You go back to your old favorite,'' she finished for him.

He nodded, then his smile dropped. ''Are we talking about the same thing?''

Suddenly anxious to end the meeting, she stood and extended her left hand out of respect for his left-handedness. ''I appreciate your offer to give me another chance, Mr. Bentley. I will take you up on it.''

Standing slowly, he shook her hand, but when

she felt needlelike pain pressing into her palm, Piper winced and released his hand abruptly.

"What's wrong?" he asked, looking at the inside of his left hand.

"You might want to check your engagement ring," she said with a faint smile, flexing her hand. "I think it's booby-trapped."

Peering more closely, his mouth tightened with irritation. "The prongs to one of the settings has pulled away." He tugged on the ring, but it wouldn't budge. His face reddened with the effort and he finally gave up with a frustrated sigh. "Damned humidity," he muttered.

"At least you don't have to worry about losing it," she said sweetly. "In this weather, it's as good as a tattoo." She led the way out of the lab, walking quickly to speed their parting, and smiled at Rich as he approached them.

After the men exchanged greetings, Rich turned to her with a wry expression in his eye. "Piper, I hope you enjoy your evening with Henry."

"I intend to," she said in her best warning voice, then shook her head at his back as he walked away.

"You didn't mention what this Henry fellow does for a living." Ian's conversational tone brought her back to the moment.

Piper weighed her options. "No, I didn't."

"Well?"

"Well, what?"

He cleared his throat mildly. "Well, what does the man do for a living?"

Her mind raced. "Henry's a businessman."

"Really? What kind of business?"

"Uh, films."

"In Mudville?"

"Well, he's sort of into distribution—he travels quite a bit."

He looked at her for a moment, then shrugged. "Listen, I'll be at the motel for another week. I might as well get in a few days of fishing before I return to Chicago." He scribbled the number on a piece of paper. "In the meantime, if you want me to drop in and sample a recipe, just call. If we come to an agreement on a product in the next couple of days, perhaps I can meet with marketing and production before I leave."

"Then you wouldn't have a reason to come back," she observed lightly.

He handed her the paper and returned his pen to his shirt pocket. "I guess not," he agreed quietly. Was that the smallest hint of regret in his voice? Ian turned to leave without saying goodbye, then snapped his fingers. "I almost forgot," he said, suddenly smiling. "I brought you something."

Piper's heart rate kicked up as she watched him lay his briefcase on her desk and flip up the latches.

Then he reached inside and withdrew a compact, black umbrella with a leather handle. "For you, Ms. Shepherd." He extended the elegant umbrella to her with a heart-pounding grin, and added, "Just in case you run out of plastic bags."

She watched him walk away, shake hands with a couple of passersby, then step onto the elevator without a backward glance. Turning the umbrella over in her hands, she recalled all too well their fateful meeting. A sad smile curved her mouth. Had things turned out differently between them, the incident might have made an interesting story to tell her own granddaughter some day.

By lunchtime, Piper decided to take the afternoon off—she could brainstorm better in her own kitchen than in the lab anyway. And it would give her plenty of time to get ready for her dinner date with Henry. Perhaps a lengthy ritual would assuage some of the guilt she felt at not being more excited about spending the evening with him.

When she pulled into the driveway, she saw Lenny lying shirtless in a hammock between two small trees in his mother's tiny front yard. The trees themselves were fairly buckling under the strain of his dead weight. He appeared to be snoozing, so she emerged from her van as quietly as possible and tiptoed around the side of her house.

"Hey, Piper, what's shakin'?" he croaked.

Piper groaned and turned back to watch him struggle to stand. The trees bowed violently with his efforts. Suddenly the hammock twisted and flipped, catapulting him facedown into the grass. Piper gasped in dismay and trotted back to see if he was hurt.

"Len." She shook his bare shoulder and experienced a stab of alarm when he didn't immediately respond. "Len," she said louder, shaking him harder.

He stirred and lifted his head, moaning.

Her shoulders sagged in relief. "Len, it's Piper. Are you okay?"

The expression on his grass-stained face was one of confusion. "Where am I?"

Piper rolled her eyes heavenward. As if he could be anywhere but at his mother's house, doing nothing. Even amnesia couldn't stamp out a lifetime habit. "You fell out of your hammock, Len. Can you move?"

He spit out a few blades of grass. "I think so." He slowly raised himself on his elbows, and with her help pushed himself to his bare feet. Moving gingerly, he tested his limbs and turned his head from side to side. "I guess I'm okay," he said, sounding relieved.

Piper smiled. "I'm glad, Len—*aarggghh!*" Before she knew it, he'd yanked her to him in an awkward embrace and kissed her full on the lips. He tasted like grass and sweat, and she wrenched away from him angrily, wiping her mouth. Lenny took a half step backward, fright evident on his face.

Furious, she went after him, pummeling him with her purse, first right, then left, to punctuate her words. "What — do — you — think — you — are — *doing?*"

He held up his hands in meek defense. "I'm sorry, Piper, I'm sorry!"

She stopped and jammed her hands on her hips. "Just make sure it doesn't happen again."

He pulled a sad face, crossing his arms and staring at the ground. "I saw you kissing that city fella last night in your kitchen, so I figured I'd better step in and stake my claim."

Her eyebrows shot up. "You were spying on me?"

Lenny looked indignant. "No, I wasn't!"

She nodded. "You were spying on me!"

Flustered, he sputtered, "Well, you opened your window, so I figured you meant for me to see— that you were trying to make me jealous."

*"Jealous?"* Piper pressed her lips together to keep herself from saying something that would hurt the man's feelings. After a deep, calming breath, she said, "Lenny, I wasn't trying to make you jeal-

ous. You and I are just…friends. I don't think of you in a…romantic way.''

A wounded expression settled on his green face. "You don't?"

She shook her head kindly. ''No, I don't. But I'm sure there are lots of women around Mudville who would like to go out with you.''

He grinned, revealing a blade of grass between his front teeth. ''You think?''

Piper stared, hesitating. ''Well…sure, Len. Of course, it might help if you, say, got a job?''

His forehead creased and he chewed on his lip, deep in concentration.

''Or maybe got a place of your own?''

Lenny's eyes widened and he pursed his mouth, as if he'd never considered the possibility until now.

''And maybe—'' she gestured vaguely toward his ragged black denim shorts ''—put on some clothes?''

He scratched his belly and nodded, warming up to the idea. ''Don Langley told me he could use someone to work the pumps at the Gas Giddyup.''

She smiled and lifted her hand in the air. ''There you go.''

A slow smile lifted his face. ''Yeah, maybe you're right, Piper.''

Glancing at her watch, she said, "I'll bet you've got time to shower and get down there today."

"Yeah," he said, grinning. "I'll give it a try."

"Good luck. I'll see you later." She patted him on the shoulder and walked back to her house, expelling a long breath. Once inside, she immediately sorted through a box of linens her grandmother had given her until she found a white opaque curtain panel, which she threaded through a spring-loaded café rod and hung in the kitchen window next to the table. She stood on the chair Ian had occupied and tried not to remember the hungry way he had looked at her, the sexy way he had pulled her to him and the earth-shattering way he had kissed her. Her hands trembled just thinking about him.

Piper climbed down on shaky knees and leaned forward on the table, taking comfort in the smooth, worn wood beneath her fingers. Somehow, she was going to have to get the image of Ian out of her head. She'd barely slept last night, and she didn't want her distraction to ruin what could be the beginning of a perfectly satisfying relationship with Henry Walden.

To keep her hands busy, she fixed a BLT sandwich and opened the two boxes of kitchen supplies her grandmother had given her. Slowly she unpacked a drawerful of obscure and little-used gadgets like shish-kebab skewers, melon scoopers and corn-on-the-cob holders, remembering exactly which drawers they had occupied in her grandmother's wonderful-smelling kitchen.

When she uncovered a stack of aprons, Piper squealed with delight. Since most of the garments were handmade from old cotton feedsack bags, they were faded and limp from countless washings. All of them she'd recalled her grandmother wearing on various occasions. She buried her face in the fabric and inhaled the sweet, clean smell of lemon-scented detergent and line-drying.

In the second box were canned goods and half-used but perfectly good containers of nonperishables. She opened her already crowded cabinets and rearranged packages to make room for pasta, flour, cornstarch, baking soda, rice, oats and a wide assortment of once-popular cooking ingredients she'd probably never use. Such as the dry malted-milk mix, she thought, shaking her head ruefully. Piper wedged the box between a package of dried beans and a bag of miniature sugar cubes, then stopped.

Malted milk. Lights exploded in her head as ideas tumbled into her mind faster than she could process them. A malted-milk chocolate cake with some wonderfully decadent icing—no, a sauce, a goopy frothy sauce reminiscent of old-time malted shakes. No—two sauces, one a rich, thick dark chocolate sauce to add just a tang of bittersweet. In her mind, she could see the sauces dripping over the edge of the cake, pooling in the bottom of a bowl-like dish, swirling together like...a mud puddle.

Barely able to contain her excitement, she rummaged for a sheet of paper and something to write with. In a junk drawer she found a napkin and a brown felt-tip marker and wrote *Mississippi Malted Mud Puddle.*

Then she opened a scrapbook of recipes she'd stolen, begged and borrowed over the years. She could picture the recipe card she was searching for, she simply couldn't remember when she'd last seen it or used it. After two trips through the scrapbook, front to back, at last she found the yellowed card: Granny Falkner's No-Fail Chocolate Cake. Piper ran her finger down the list of ingredients, changing the quantity of dry components to allow for the malt, and altering the wet ingredients to accommodate one of her own favorite touches: coffee to enhance the flavor of the chocolate.

For luck, she donned one of her granny's aprons, then preheated the oven. Soon, she was splattered and dusted with wet and dry ingredients. Since her rash had finally disappeared, Piper tasted sparingly, trusting her nose to guide her in finding the best combination of flavorings. When the oven beeped, she pondered what kind of pan to use. Squatting on the floor in front of her crowded cabinet of miscellaneous bakeware, she spied another one of her grandmother's castoffs: a giant muffin pan. Piper prepared the pan and spooned in the thick batter. At the last minute, she hollowed out a depression in the top of each muffin, then slid the pan inside the oven. Carefully, she closed the door and wiped her hands on her apron.

"Prepare to be wowed, Mr. Bentley."

"JUST TELL HER I called," Ian said. "Again." He returned the phone to its cradle and sighed. He'd tried to get in touch with Meredith every day. Her assistant assured him she was simply swamped with meetings and traveling, but he was beginning to become concerned.

Yet he had to admit to himself that he needed to hear Meredith's voice for his own selfish reasons— to remind him of all the good times they'd had. And to clear his head of the confusing images of Piper Shepherd that left him lying awake at night on sweat-soaked sheets.

While changing into casual clothes, the wayward prong on his ring snagged his dress shirt and ripped a hole in the sleeve. He cursed and stomped to the bathroom, determined to remove the band. He squirted shampoo around it and tugged until it popped over his knuckle. The ring bounced into the sink and headed for the drain, sending his heart to his throat. "No!" he shouted, and covered the drain just as the ring fell safely onto the back of his hand.

Weak with relief, he dried the ring and shoved it back onto his finger. Tight and troublesome was better than lost. Besides, he told himself sternly, he might have to get used to wearing it.

Quickly he pulled on jeans, T-shirt and tennis shoes, then headed toward the lake he'd discovered earlier in the week. Four hours and several hundred dollars' worth of equipment later, he'd caught nine catfish and released them all since he didn't have the means to prepare them. He'd been tempted to string them and take them to Piper, but even *he* recognized the idea as a thinly disguised ploy to see her again.

Ian left the lake and retraced the path to the wonderful old house he'd told Benjamin about. The real-estate agent had faxed his partner photos, along with a plat showing surrounding farmland. Benjamin had made an offer right away, but the owner hadn't responded.

If anything, Ian's admiration expanded as he drove up the curving driveway. The house stood as a grande dame, dressed in white limestone with black shutters, overlooking a valley of crisscrossing fields that resembled an Americana portrait. Ian himself was completely taken with the place, and

the thought scurried across his mind that it would
be a wonderful place to raise children. Finding an
opening, his mind wandered farther out of bounds
than he'd ever permitted. He tried to picture Meredith puttering in the flower beds with toddlers at
her knees… He scoffed at his ridiculous musings—
Meredith, dirt and children? Never.

Without warning, Piper's face emerged to replace
Meredith's, except this time he didn't laugh. Instead, a warm, syrupy feeling descended over him.
For some odd reason, he could easily picture Piper
as mistress of this house.

He pulled to a stop by an ivy-covered mailbox
and climbed out slowly, stretching his legs. It
wasn't until he'd closed the car door and taken two
steps toward the walk that he realized a slim, elderly woman had risen from her rocking chair,
craning her neck to get a good look at him. He was
in luck, he decided. Maybe the owner would give
him a tour. "Hello," he called.

"Hello," she said, offering him a tentative smile.
Something about her expression struck a memory
chord, but he decided the woman reminded him of
his own grandmother.

"Nice day," he offered as he drew closer. The
woman held a needlepoint canvas she'd apparently
been working on.

"Yes, it is. Can I help you?"

"Yes, ma'am. My name is Ian Bentley—I'm from Chicago. A colleague of mine in Boston by the name of Benjamin Warner has made an offer on your house, and I wondered if I might see the inside for myself."

The woman angled her head at him. "Bentley, did you say?"

"Yes, ma'am. Ian Bentley."

She smiled an invitation. "Come right in, Mr. Bentley. Would you like a cold glass of lemonade?"

"MERCY." Henry whistled low as he stepped inside Piper's door, studying the contours of her short, black dress as if he wanted to personally undo each of the center buttons that held it together from collar to hem. The thought entered her head that she wished she was wearing the dress for Ian, but she sent the notion on its way.

Henry leaned jauntily against the door frame, flexed his exposed biceps and gave her a leering smile. "You know, Piper, we could always get a pizza delivered." He jerked his head toward the monster four-wheel-drive truck he'd driven into her tiny yard, stopping inches from her petunias. "I brought a couple of good flicks with me." He lowered his chin and his voice. "And one of them I ain't even allowed to rent, if you know what I mean.''

She smiled tightly and fastened the button just above her cleavage. "I can guess... But maybe next time, Henry. Tonight I kind of had my heart set on dinner.''

He made a regretful noise with his dimpled cheek, then shrugged. "Then let's get going.''

She managed to fasten two more buttons while she grabbed her purse, leaving only the topmost button undone. Outside, Piper eyed the high-rise truck he'd driven, wondering how on earth she could climb up wearing this dress. And her ankle felt weak because she'd removed the bandage for the occasion. She unbuttoned the last few buttons near her hem, hoping to prevent a seam blowout. Abruptly, Henry scooped her into his arms and dumped her unceremoniously into the seat, then slammed the door.

Righting herself as much as possible, Piper watched her date saunter around to the driver's side. He gave her a devilish grin as he swung himself up into his seat, and she recalled Janet's warnings about Henry's reputation as a lady-killer. She had to admit, though, he was handsome in a very two-hundred-fifty-watt kind of way. He positively glowed, and she had a disturbing image of him oiling down his tanned skin prior to their date. Sure enough, the steering wheel bore shiny fingerprints. It suddenly occurred to her that Henry's video store sat next to a tanning salon and the chances he'd gotten that golden glow doing yard work were slim to none.

"I thought we'd go to the steak house," he said. "They have a buffet tonight. All you can eat for seven ninety-five."

"Fine," she said, trying to look enthusiastic, then chastised herself. It certainly wasn't Henry's fault there were so few nice places to eat in the area. In fact, the steak house, which lay a few miles down the interstate outside of Mudville, was actually one of the nicest. "As a matter of fact, I haven't had a good steak in a long time," she added, determined to put a good spin on the situation.

Henry seemed satisfied, and roared toward the interstate. Piper shakily belted herself in. The short ride was pleasant enough. She didn't have to worry about making small talk because apparently Henry's dad's sister had been a bluegrass-music singer in the sixties and Henry was convinced he had inherited her gift. Piper had her doubts, and was glad when they pulled into the restaurant parking lot until she remembered she'd have to somehow get down.

Henry was one step ahead of her, though. As he lifted her down, sliding her against his body until her sandaled feet touched the ground, she wondered if he drove the monster truck simply for the privilege of loading and unloading his female passengers. She nervously smiled her thanks and stepped back out of his muscle-bound arms.

Word of the steak house's all-you-can-eat buffet must have gotten around, Piper decided, because the place was crowded for a weeknight. Country music blared over speakers and Henry hummed along as they were shown to a table. He winked at the young waitress before she flitted away, and Piper frowned into her menu.

Henry sat with his arms crossed on the table, and glanced around the restaurant, as if looking for someone more interesting than Piper. "Do you already know what you want?" she asked.

He glanced back to her and started bobbing his neck like a rooster in time to the song coming over the speakers. "Yep. A bloody steak and the buffet."

She watched him, suddenly wishing she'd gone along with the pizza idea. God only knew who they might run into—her boss, her grandmother's friends—

"Ms. Shepherd, what a nice surprise."

Piper's stomach somersaulted as she spotted Ian striding toward them. She looked around frantically for a table to dive under, then realized with a sink-ing heart that she had no choice but to suffer through an introduction.

"Mr. Bentley," she acknowledged him coolly. He looked devastating in jeans and a cream-colored short-sleeve shirt. And he seemed happier than any time since she'd met him.

"You know this guy?" Henry asked her, narrowing his eyes at Ian.

"Piper and I work together," Ian said smoothly, extending his big hand toward the blond man. "Ian Bentley."

"Henry Walden."

"Oh, yes, *Henry,*" Ian said. "Piper told me all about you."

Piper set her jaw and Henry's pale eyebrows arrowed up. "She did?"

Ian nodded enthusiastically.

Piper wrapped her hand around the steak knife in front of her, and gauged the distance between her hand and Ian's chest.

A corner of Henry's mouth went up and she could see his confidence flooding back as he glanced her way with a smirk, then back to Ian. "And just what did Piper tell you?"

"Mr. Bentley," she cut in none too gently. "If you don't mind, Henry and I would really like to be alone." Piper ignored Henry's look of surprise.

Ian looked contrite. "Where are my manners?

Mr. Walden, perhaps I'll see you another time and we can discuss the fascinating business you're in."

"Sure," Henry said, sitting back and puffing out his chest. "In fact—" he reached into the pocket of his sleeveless shirt and withdrew a slip of bright orange paper "—here you go."

Mortification washed over Piper as Ian scanned the paper.

Ian looked enormously pleased as he shook Henry's hand. "Gee, thanks, Mr. Walden—a free rental."

Piper poked her tongue into her cheek and glanced up at Ian with loathing.

"See you soon, Piper." He saluted, then retired to a table a few feet away, just behind Henry's right shoulder, never taking his eyes off her. He grinned broadly as he held up the rental coupon, then gave her a thumbs-up.

"Seems like a nice guy," Henry observed.

"Looks are deceiving," Piper said, seething.

He grinned. "So you were talking about me, eh?"

She didn't know what to say, so she gave him a noncommittal smile and took a sip of water.

The waitress skipped back to the table with water and tea, and a sly smile for Henry. Piper ordered a small steak, medium-well, even though her appetite had vanished. She scooted her chair around until

Henry's arms blocked her view of Ian. When Henry left to visit the buffet, Ian seemed to be enjoying his meal, smiling up at the young waitress who had earlier flirted with Henry. Piper watched him under her lashes, pretending to read the fact-filled paper place mat.

When Henry returned with a laden plate, she made painful, strained small talk until their orders arrived. He ate like a wolf and talked with his mouth full. Piper could only manage to choke down a couple of bites of the meat. She couldn't wait to get home—alone. At last he had eaten his fill, and they were ready to leave. Coincidentally, Ian was walking out at the same time.

"Did you enjoy your dinner?" he asked them in a friendly voice.

Henry belched and nodded. Piper turned her back and kept moving toward the truck, already dreading being slung into the seat. But Henry, undoubtedly trying to improve his chances for more than just a good-night kiss, clasped her around the waist and lifted her with infinite slowness onto the seat. Too late, she realized her knees were nearly at his eye level and he had a bird's-eye view up her dress.

"Nice," he said, abandoning subtlety. He glanced around in the semidarkness and Piper panicked when she realized he was going to make a move on her behind the protection of his truck door.

When he looked back to her, his mouth was slack and his eyes hooded. "Real nice." He slid his hands between her knees like a diver cutting through water, heading for the finish line.

She stiffened and jammed her knees together while pushing his hands away. "Don't touch me!" she barked.

But Henry only laughed, a lazy, throaty laugh. "Come on, Piper," he whispered. "This seat is just made for showing me what you got—I'll make you feel good." His hands zoomed forward again and Piper, furious, lifted her foot and kicked him in the chest, propelling him backward. He landed on his back with an oomph, and Piper glanced around wildly, wanting to run but deciding she had more leverage at this height if he came back for more.

"Take me home, Henry," she said through clenched teeth. "Now."

He sprang to his feet and brushed off his backside, then advanced on her again with a nasty smile. "Oh, you're a little tiger, aren't you—hey!"

Piper's eyes widened to see that Ian had Henry in some kind of choke hold with his arm yanked up behind him.

Henry bucked around uselessly, grimacing. "Hey, let me go!"

A stone-faced Ian looked at her and nodded toward the parking lot. "Piper, get in my car. I'm taking you home."

"But I..." She trailed off when common sense prevailed, and climbed down. She sidled around the two men and walked toward Ian's car. She turned back to see him release Henry by shoving him to the ground, facefirst. She couldn't tell what Ian said to him, but Henry didn't move. She did, however, see Ian remove a little slip of orange paper from his shirt pocket and toss it near Henry's head.

Still looking grim, Ian strode toward her and unlocked the passenger-side door.

"Ian, I—"

"Get in the car," he said, nodding.

She frowned. "I just wanted to say thanks."

His expression softened and he smiled. "Oh. You're welcome."

Afraid he was going to kiss her on the spot, Piper ducked inside.

Tension fogged the interior of the car until her ears felt plugged. They were nearly a mile down the road before either one of them spoke. Tingling with humiliation, she shifted in her seat. "I'm glad I ran into you."

"Me, too."

She laughed nervously. "Because you'll never guess—I had a breakthrough today at home and I came up with the best chocolate cake you'll ever eat.''

"You baked the cake at home?''

"Yeah,'' she said, staring out the window. "I was going to bring it into the office tomorrow and call you, but...''

"But since I'm taking you home anyway...''

"I could offer you a little preview.''

He was silent for so long Piper finally opened her mouth to recant her half-baked invitation, but before she did, he said, "I think that's a great idea. Funny, I just realized, I'm still hungry.''

Their gazes locked in the dark and Piper shivered. Once they arrived home, she would close the curtains, take the phone off the hook—anything to keep them from being interrupted during their... dessert.

# CHAPTER NINE

*No man will buy the cow if he can get the milk free.*

IAN FOLLOWED PIPER as they entered her house through the back door. She turned on a night-light above the sink, casting a low glow over the small room. Next to the trilling, chirping insects outside, the house seemed eerily quiet, the silence broken only by the hum of the refrigerator, the almost staticky noise of the cloying humidity and the bass thudding of his heart.

Forget the dessert, he wanted *her,* he admitted unabashedly as he raked his gaze over her full-body profile. The black sleeveless dress molded to her curves, stopping midthigh on her bare, tanned legs. Black strappy sandals revealed pink-painted toes. Beautiful. She had dominated his thoughts all evening—hell, since the moment he met her, if truth be known.

Her hands shook, he noticed, as she switched on a saucer-size fan sitting on the counter. Her hair blew back slightly from her face as the fan's oscillating head passed over her. From the droop of her shoulders, she was either scared, or doubtful—or both—of what might happen before he left. The linoleum squeaked beneath his shoes as he walked up behind her. He slid his hands around her narrow waist, splaying his fingers over her stomach, and inhaled deeply behind her ear as he gently pulled her back against him.

Piper gasped, covering his hands with hers and arching into him. Absurdly, he was already dreading the morning. This might be their only time together, ever. He turned her around in his arms and kissed her, moving his lips against hers in a slow, sensual ravage. Using his tongue, he probed with an intensity that promised later intimacies. He moaned in gratification when she sucked the column of his tongue, making pledges of her own.

She exhaled puffs of hot air that he drew in and swallowed, wanting to possess the very essence of her. Her body fit against his perfectly and his hands itched to undo every one of those buttons that stood between her body and his gaze, her skin and his mouth. At last he lifted his head. Her eyes shone in the shadows.

"I've wanted you," he murmured, "since I saw you lying there in a puddle of water in the parking lot."

She laughed softly, then pushed gently at his chest. "Speaking of puddles…my cake!"

"Piper," he said, laughing and grabbing her hands. "You're not serious about having dessert, are you?"

"Yes," she declared, pouting and pulling away. She pulled a pan forward and peeled back a napkin that had been covering the cakes. "Wha-lah!"

He moved in behind her again, nibbling the back of her neck. "And I thought that was you that smelled so good. Wait a minute—" he sniffed her temple "—it *is* you."

"Ian," she protested weakly. "It'll just take me a minute to warm up the sauce—you're going to love this, I know."

He sighed noisily. "Only if you'll split it with me."

"That's the idea—a dessert to share." Pointing to the table, she ordered, "Sit."

"Yes, ma'am." On the way, he spotted an aged radio on top of the refrigerator, circa 1960. "Nice. Does it work?"

"Hmm? Oh, yeah, but you might have to play with it a little."

*Might as well play with something,* he thought. Ian flipped the power button and turned the knob all the way left, then all the way right until strains of Marvin Gaye drifted over their heads. "Perfect," he pronounced. Since her hips started swaying to the sensual beat, he assumed she agreed.

Relegated to the table, he sat down and watched her remove two bowls, presumably the sauces, from the refrigerator. She placed one bowl in the microwave, then rummaged in an overhead cabinet, giving him a nice glimpse of upper thigh. His body tightened and he gritted his teeth. Sitting out of range of the light and in near darkness, he drummed his fingers restlessly against the smooth surface of the table. "Anything I can do?"

"Do you want some coffee?"

He shook his head. "But you know what sounds good? A tall glass of water."

She grinned and pointed her elbow at the refrigerator. "Use the bottled water—it tastes better. I'll have a glass, too."

While he pulled glasses from the cupboard and filled them from the water container, he watched her assemble the dessert with her small hands. She placed what appeared to be a large muffin with a sinkhole in the top, on a deep saucerlike dish with fluted edges. The heavy scent of chocolate, rich and nose-tingling, wafted around her. Carefully, she drizzled an unheated frothy sauce into the center until it oozed over the sides. She licked her fingers, causing him to set his jaw. Then she removed the bowl from the microwave and repeated the drizzling and the oozing with what appeared to be a thin, dark chocolate sauce.

"Looks delicious," he said, clasping her wrist. He lifted her hand to his mouth and licked the black chocolate from the tips of two fingers. When he released her, he grinned. "The cake looks good, too."

Her eyes looked slightly glazed, and Ian wondered if they'd be able to make it all the way through dessert before tearing off each other's clothes. He carried their glasses to the table and sat down heavily. She followed, her high-heeled sandals tapping against the floor. She set the cake between the two glasses and he reached for her.

"Do we get to eat with our hands?" he teased.

She eluded him with a sidestep and veered back to the counter. "No," she scoffed, holding up two spoons. "And here's extra sauce—hot and cold." She set the cold and warm toppings on the table. "Whipped cream?"

"Sure," he said, swallowing.

She opened the refrigerator. "Cherries, too?"

The woman was killing him. "Why not?"

She carried her loot to the table, removed the lids and claimed the other chair. "Well, dig in."

He reached for her again, but she whacked him on the back of the hand with a spoon, so he decided to behave...for the time being. "What is it, exactly?" he asked, scooping up a dripping mouthful.

"See if you can guess." She chewed on her lower lip in the most delicious way.

The flavor of the cake flowed pleasingly over this tongue, and he glanced down, impressed. "Mmm. Let's see, I know that taste...it's malt."

Piper nodded and leaned her elbow on the table. "Do you like it?"

"It's great," he admitted, lowering his spoon for another bite. "Have a bite." He held a spoonful to her lips. She hesitated for only a second, then opened her small mouth. He gently inserted the spoon, but still managed to dribble sauce on her chin.

He stopped her hand in midair. "Let me." When she swallowed, he leaned forward and licked the sauce from her chin, nipping along her jaw. Reaching past her, he found the bowl of dark chocolate and dipped his finger.

Ian lifted his hand and stroked the chocolate down the side of her neck. "Oh, look," he murmured, then dipped his head and licked off the streak, inch by delectable inch. The dessert abandoned, he gripped her chair by the seat and dragged her closer to him in the near darkness. He dipped his finger into the cold sauce next and painted the hollow of her collarbone, lapping it up a moment later.

She moaned, swaying into him, then deftly undid the top few buttons on the little black dress with her fingers, giving him a glimpse of her lacy black bra and the hollow between her breasts. He crushed her to him, burying his face in her cleavage. His body leaped in response to her beauty and her curves.

"Piper," he whispered against her skin. "I want to make love to you."

She moaned in acquiescence, digging her hands into his hair, pressing his mouth against her. He dragged his tongue across the top of her breasts, then lifted his head and kissed her hard on the mouth. Throbbing with need, he twisted and set the cake and glasses safely out of harm's way on the counter.

Then in one motion, he stood and lifted her from the chair onto the table, standing between her spread knees, the dress straining at the lower buttons. He made short work of them, freeing her legs to open wider, revealing toned thighs and black panties. Groaning, he wrapped one arm around her back and pulled her sex against his with one hand, while freeing the rest of the buttons with the other.

"Ambidextrous," she mumbled, arching her back.

"Hmm?"

"You're ambidextrous."

He smiled as the dress fell open, revealing her bra, her narrow waist and shallow navel, and the skimpiest pair of panties he'd ever seen. "Comes in handy sometimes." He pulled her mouth to his in a grinding kiss and pushed the dress down over her shoulders.

She unbuttoned his shirt and slipped her hands inside to thumb his nipples. Ian sucked in a sharp breath and shrugged out of his shirt, letting it fall to the floor. She tugged at the waist of his jeans, but he stopped her, knowing he had to pace himself, wanting to prolong her pleasure.

Sweeping the dress from beneath her, he pressed her back on the table, feasting on the sight of her hills and valleys in the shallow light. Slender and fine-boned, she was simply incredible. Wildly anxious to see her naked, he forced himself to slow down. He dipped his fingers into the sauces and painted cold and warm squiggles across the tops of her breasts, over her rib cage, down her flat tummy and into her navel, then licked, sucked and nibbled it off, working in reverse. He paused at her mouth for a deep, bittersweet-chocolate kiss, but her clutching hands skimming over his bare chest sent him seeking other erogenous zones.

Reaching beneath her, he unfastened the flimsy

bra, freeing her breasts. Ian nearly fell apart just from the sight of her nipples, dark pink buds in the center of tan lines left by a skimpy bikini. He leaned over her and touched his tongue to a tender tip and she bucked beneath him. Her skin felt silken against his cheek.

He held her hands above her head, clasping her wrists loosely. He laved one breast and latched on to her nipple, drawing it into his mouth, eliciting mewling noises from her throat. Half lying, half standing, he pressed the ridge of his erection against her open thighs.

Impulsively, he lifted the bowl of warm dark chocolate and dribbled it over her firm round breasts and lower, to pool around her navel. He lapped the sticky sweetness from her navel first, dipping in his tongue, rimming the edge, then ate his way back to the other breast, where he feasted anew.

When her skin glowed clean and moist, he kissed his way down to her waist, then ran his fingers around the lacy waistband of her panties. Stepping back, he lifted her hips and dragged off her panties, letting them fall from his fingers to join his shirt on the floor.

Ian allowed himself one sweeping, mouth-drying gaze at her body, and nearly came undone. She lay on the table with her head and arms thrown back, looking at him through thick lashes. Her breasts jutted in the air, glistening from the bath he'd given them. The inward curve of her waist sloped into the outward curve of her hip with perfection that could only be found in nature. High-cut bathing-suit bottoms had left a V of pale skin at the fork of her thighs, outlining the center of her desire. She had one knee slightly raised, which Ian kissed while he slipped off her sandals.

Mesmerized by her beauty, Ian reached for the open jar of maraschino cherries and tipped it to the side, drenching the tangle of dark curls between her thighs with the cold red juice. One perfect stemmed cherry slipped out and bounced against her nest, lingering there. She jerked spasmodically as the liquid pooled and traveled down the channel of her sex, dripping from her and onto the table.

A neat person at the core, Ian bent to catch the remaining juice with his tongue.

Piper felt like a bowl of melting ice cream, losing her hard edges and firm boundaries and simply flowing to meet whatever she happened to encounter. She didn't think Ian could tease another nerve ending, could push another button, until she felt his hot breath on her thighs and his tongue removing the red, sticky sauce from her most sensitive folds.

She yelled his name, and raised her arms above her head, searching for something to grab on to.

Encountering the wall, she pushed against it, moving against his tongue. He lifted one leg and draped it over his shoulder, then probed her entrance with his fingers. With a sudden thrust of his arm, he filled her, massaging her, making love to her with his hand while removing the vestiges of the cherry syrup with long, hard strokes of his tongue.

Piper remembered enough about sex to know she'd never had an orgasm like the one building in her loins. She felt totally wanton and selfish, wanting and needing the release only he could deliver. He moaned against her skin and hummed on the tender nub of her control, playing her like a mouth instrument. She urged him on with as much encouragement as she could form in her throat. As she drew near the pinnacle, she relied on guttural noises and frantic hip thrusts to let him know she was zooming closer. With two slashes of his plundering tongue, he sent her sailing over the edge. She convulsed around his fingers, and against his mouth, gasping his name, clawing at the wall behind her. He coaxed her down with soft strokes and soothing noises, withdrawing his fingers gently and kissing her sensitive thighs.

His hands snaked behind her and slowly pulled her upright into a sitting position. In his teeth, he held the single cherry and offered her half in a slow juicy kiss. On his tongue she tasted chocolate, cherries and her own musk, a heady mix. She pressed her breasts against the width of his chest, reveling in the firm wall of muscle across his back. Wrapping her legs around his hips, she pulled herself to the edge of the table, gasping when the fabric of his jeans brushed against her sensitive, engorged skin.

She reached around and ran her hands underneath the waistband of his boxers, squeezing his buttocks. When she put her hands on the snap below his flat stomach, he put his hand over hers.

"Piper," he whispered, "don't do this unless you are absolutely sure."

A shiver ran through her, despite the heat and their fevered skin. "I'm sure," she answered, and unzipped his jeans. He kicked off his shoes, and she pushed his jeans down over his thighs. He dragged them down his legs, then stepped out of them. His pale boxers did nothing to hide his fabric-straining erection.

She greedily pulled down his waistband to free his arousal, the sight of his rigid member sending new moisture to dampen the wood beneath her. Clasping him firmly with both hands, she fell against him in a deep kiss, stroking him until beads of his moisture flowed down over her fingers.

Pushing against his chest, she slid down his body until her feet touched the floor, then she urged him backward, until he had to sit in the chair she'd abandoned. As he sat, she fell to her knees, bringing the chocolate with her.

She scooped up a palmful of the warm, sticky sauce and slathered it on his straining member in long, milking strokes. He watched her with hooded eyes, and when she leaned forward to take him into her mouth, she saw his eyes roll back in ecstasy. She had never pleased a man with her mouth, and she loved it—the power to bring him to the brink, and let him ebb away, only to bring him closer the next time. He kneaded her shoulders, gasping and groaning through clenched teeth, while she devoured him.

"Piper. Now—I need to make love to you now."

He stood and carried her, setting her on the table, then stooped and fished his wallet out of his jeans. With hurried hands, he removed a condom, ripped open the package and rolled it on. Panting heavily, he held the small of her back with one hand and positioned himself at her entrance with his other. She was so slick with fulfillment and renewed need, he entered her with one massive thrust. Piper gasped, then groaned her pleasure as he filled her completely. Wrapping her arms and legs around him, she followed his rhythm lead, her body already tuned for another explosion.

He was a vocal lover, and she found his throaty

exclamations an incredible turn-on. His hands never stilled during their lovemaking—he ran his fingers over her back and hips, into her hair, over her throat and neck and face. As his thrusts became quicker and harder, Piper felt her body start to hum. He responded to her frantic noises by shifting her backward slightly and caressing her nipples while plunging into her deep and hard.

The orgasm hit her like the flash from a camera, startling and lingering. She cried his name over and over. When his own noises escalated, she urged him home. The muscles in his shoulders and stomach bunched, then he shuddered and gasped her name, his expression an intense mixture of pleasure and pain.

In the few seconds of his utmost vulnerability, of his wild abandon, Piper felt a poignant loss, because during those few seconds, she loved Ian. For that moment in time, he wasn't a virtual stranger from halfway across the country who would never accept someone like her into his life, and she wasn't a lonely old maid who felt more affinity for a limestone house than for her own mother. For that moment in time, they were two star-crossed lovers who evoked extraordinary passion in each other, passion that overrode rationality and reason.

When he finally opened his eyes, he was smiling, and Piper quickly followed suit, relieved he had enjoyed their lovemaking as much as she had. He kissed a trail across her shoulder, then whispered, "I could sure go for that tall glass of water now."

Her laughter resounded in the room and they disentangled themselves.

"Do you have to leave?" she asked, trying to sound casual.

"No."

Her heart and body soared, although after his performance, she certainly didn't expect an encore. "Okay, then follow me."

He snatched the glasses while she grabbed a handful of their clothes, then he followed her to her bedroom. Their bare feet padding against the wooden floor struck Piper as being so intimate, she would probably never forget the sound. Inside the bedroom, she turned on a lamp.

Ian glanced around the room and pronounced, "Nice."

She smiled her thanks. Like every room in her house, her bedroom was small, but bright and uncluttered.

"Oh, I left something in the kitchen." He set down the glasses, then disappeared.

Piper slowly draped their clothes over the back of a chair, then turned down her bed, wondering if he already regretted their lovemaking. Perhaps he stood in the kitchen now, scrambling to find a graceful exit after he'd had a few minutes to consider their lapse. She walked into the bathroom and took a two-minute shower to rinse the remnants of the sweet sauces from her body. After sorting through her sleepwear, she pulled on red tap pants and a camisole. But with her hand on the bathroom doorknob, she stopped, worried she looked too expectant. Oh, well, since she'd broken almost every rule in her grandmother's manhunting book, she'd have to wing the rest of it, too.

Still naked, Ian stood draining the glass of water when she walked in.

He glanced at her outfit and frowned. "Oh, I wish you hadn't done that."

"You don't like my pajamas?"

"No, I meant take a shower."

Confused, she asked, "Why?"

"Because," he said earnestly, "I forgot the whipped cream." He raised the can, shook it and walked toward her with a mischievous glint in his eye.

# CHAPTER TEN

*Don't fret if it doesn't work out—there's more than one man for every woman, else the odds of finding him would be astronomical.*

PIPER HAD THE SENSE that something was terribly wrong even before she opened her eyes. She hovered in a languid, sleepy state, delaying the inevitable moment of fully waking. A deep groan near her ear ended her semiconscious procrastination, and her eyes fluttered open in the predawn light.

Her body felt hot, sweaty even, and a little sticky under the sheet over her breasts. She lay on her right side, facing the pale wood dresser she had painstakingly refinished over several months. Big, solid pieces of furniture gave her comfort because they made her feel rooted. Trendy, disposable furniture was for flighty people—temporary people who moved around a lot and didn't get attached to things, like her mother. The two-hundred-fifty pound, intricately carved dresser was going nowhere on a whim. Piper loved waking up every morning and seeing the product of her hard work and stick-to-itiveness.

But not this morning. Because while in front of her sat evidence of long-suffering devotion, behind her lay evidence of subjugation to irrational desires.

Ian's arm lay loosely around her waist, the dark hair on his thick forearms incongruous against the pale, flowered sheet. His shallow, uneven breathing told her that he, too, was nearly awake, but not quite. Their bodies touched in a half-dozen intimate places, alarmingly familiar to her now.

The tingle of an itch traveled across her stomach. Too late, she realized her skin was reacting to last night's chocolate exchange—as if remembering the erotic intimacies she'd shared with this man was simply not enough to torture her for untold days. She'd never been driven to do anything so uninhibited in all her life. So why would she give herself with such abandon to a virtual stranger who had none of the qualities she'd set out to find—small-town, dependable, *loyal?*

Her gaze darted down to his ring finger, her eyes widening when she saw it was bare. Had he removed the ring out of respect to her, or out of respect to his lover? She gritted her teeth—perhaps he always removed it when he cheated. Remorse flooded over her like a wave of boiling water. How utterly stupid could she be?

A sickening question settled in the pit of her stomach… How many times had her mother faced the sunrise in a similar situation? Piper remembered countless mornings men had stumbled from their apartment in a state of undress, many of the losers sporting wedding rings. Her stomach turned over— had her father been a married man cheating on his wife with her mother? And even though Ian wasn't yet married, did that really make her any better than her mother? She had known his heart was committed elsewhere, and she'd slept with him anyway… Correction—it had gone way beyond sleeping, she reminded herself wryly.

And she still needed the man's business.

Mortification surged through her body, suffocating her. Frantic, she pulled away from him and swung her feet to the floor, ignoring his sleepy protests. The flimsy pajamas she'd worn to bed lay in a heap on the floor, but she bypassed them and strode straight into the bathroom. Without looking back, she closed the door quietly and lifted her long terry-cloth robe from the hook. Despite the temperature and humidity, she shrugged inside. Piper wrapped the sash tightly around her waist and leaned heavily against the door, fighting tears of frustration and regret.

She'd lost her self-respect, and with it probably the best chance she had at being able to make an offer on her grandmother's house. He'd never take her seriously when it came to business, not after last night, not after the table—oh, God... She dropped her head in her hands. What if he thought she'd seduced him in order to get his business? And what if he did offer Blythe the contract because of her irresponsible behavior? Then her bonus would be little more than payment for sexual services rendered. A sob rose in her throat, choking her.

"Piper?" A light knock on the door startled her. She straightened and inhaled sharply.

Hastily wiping tears with the heels of her hands, she sniffed and glanced in the mirror, then grabbed the sink for support. She looked like the tousled, sexed, lazy-eyed spitting image of her mother.

"Piper?" He knocked again, this time louder. "Are you okay?"

She couldn't face him, not yet. She wished she could avoid him indefinitely, but she knew that was unlikely. "Uh, yeah," she called shakily. "I'm fine. How—how about I meet you at the lab around ten-thirty?"

He was silent for a few seconds, then said, "If that's what you want." His voice had changed—was that relief? Or was he irritated she wasn't up for a morning tussle?

''That's what I want. B-before this gets more complicated and people are hurt.'' *Like me.* She turned on the shower to prevent further conversation. *Coward,* she chastised herself.

But better to be a coward, she told herself, than be doubly foolish. Because as much as she hated to admit it, if she had opened the door and he had opened his arms, she would have walked into them. Perhaps she could absolve herself someday for falling under his influence, late at night with romantic music on the radio and loneliness crowding her heart. But a meaningless tryst in the wake of morning-after insight would be unforgivable.

She heard the faint thump of a car door closing and the rumble of an engine turning over. Piper disrobed, sighing at the expanse of red, angry skin on her stomach and back, and stepped into the shower, allowing the warm water to soothe her surface discomfort.... The rest would take some time.

IAN TRIED to recall when he had last been tossed out of a woman's bed in the early-morning hours following an incredible night of mind-blowing sex, but no incidents came to mind. Which could probably be attributed to the fact that even when he'd been sowing oats as a young bachelor, he'd never indulged in such blatantly hedonistic acts as he'd shared with Piper Shepherd. He'd never finger-painted a woman with chocolate and licked it off her body gratuitously. He'd never mixed fruit with forbidden fruit. He'd never taken a woman on her kitchen table. And he'd never been so disappointed to wake up and find himself alone.

She was obviously feeling guilty over betraying Enderling, but what had prompted her to sleep with him in the first place? Was she trying to make the other man jealous? Then his gut clenched—was she trying to influence his decision about the contract? She'd been insistent that he try the dessert last night. Had it been to prime him for a meeting she'd already planned this morning? Was she perhaps in line to receive some kind of commission if he signed with Blythe? Would she threaten to take their affair public if he refused?

Pursing his mouth, Ian realized he simply had to face the possibility that she may have targeted him from the beginning—and he had been so taken by her that he'd forgone his normal scrupulous business conduct and followed her to bed. Or was her ploy furthered by some subconscious desire of his to sabotage his relationship with Meredith?

Passing a hand over his face, he groaned in frustration. He simply had to speak to Meredith today. Ian stopped and stared at his bare ring finger, panic rising in his chest. What had happened to Meredith's ring? He hadn't taken it off since his drain scare yesterday. His mind raced. When had he last seen it? Thumping his hand on the steering wheel, he fast-forwarded through last night's…scenario. He vaguely remembered his ring snagging on the pillowcase in Piper's bed, so he'd been wearing it when he went to sleep.

Muttering an oath, he jammed his hand through his hair. He'd lost Meredith's engagement ring in the twisted sheets of another woman's bed.

"GOOD MORNING," Piper said calmly. It had taken her half an hour to perfect the greeting—she wasn't so sure about what would come out of her mouth next.

"I suppose so," Ian replied, his gray eyes flitting over the most conservative outfit she owned—pale blue crepe jacket and slacks. Minus his briefcase, he still looked the part of rich businessman in a dark, single-breasted suit. His only concession to the heat was a crisp white collarless knit shirt. He held a pair of expensive-looking sunglasses in one hand. And he still wasn't wearing his ring, she noted with a jolt.

Her heart lifted with unreasonable hope, but she couldn't prevent it. Had he taken it off—and left it off—in light of their newfound attraction? Then she bit down on the inside of her cheek. Or was he simply keeping it tucked away until he returned to his lover to play the faithful partner?

He glanced around and nodded at Rich who stared, unsmiling, from a doorway just a few feet away. Her perceptive friend knew something was wrong. Ian leaned forward and lowered his voice. "I, um, seem to have left something in your house."

She frowned in confusion.

After clearing his throat, he said, "More specifically, in your bed." He wiggled the fingers on his left hand, his eyebrows raised.

His ring. He hadn't removed it—he'd *lost* it…in her bed. She might have laughed out loud if it hadn't hurt so much. Irony had her number on speed dial.

"I, um, didn't find it," she said, her gaze darting to her assistant. "Let's move this meeting into the lab, shall we?" She grabbed a blue lab coat and led the way, her feet heavy and her stomach churning. Piper tried her best to ignore Rich's pointed stare as they passed him.

Once the door to the lab had closed behind them, she wheeled. "Ian, what makes you so sure you left your ring at my house?"

His eyes widened and his head jutted forward. "What makes me so sure? How about the fact that

I was wearing it when I got there and I wasn't when I left?''

"When did you notice it was gone?'' she persisted.

He sighed. "While I was driving back to the motel before the crack of dawn. What is this—'Twenty Questions'?''

"Do you remember taking it off?''

"No, it must have come off while we were...'' His face reddened. "Sleeping.''

She crossed her arms. "Well, that certainly narrows the window of opportunity, doesn't it?''

"It probably snagged on the covers,'' he said, his voice elevated.

"*Do* you mind keeping your voice down?'' she whispered loudly. "I'd really rather everyone not know about...what happened.''

His eyebrows knitted and his eyes narrowed in anger. "Then I guess I shouldn't have waved at your neighbor this morning as I left?''

Piper moaned. "You waved at Lenny?''

A disgusted sigh left his mouth. "No, I didn't wave at anybody! What do you think, that I'm trying to advertise the fact that we slept together?''

"No,'' she said evenly. "I'm sure you're as eager as I am to keep this to ourselves.''

"Unfortunately, I'll need to come back and look for the ring.''

"I'll look for it," she promised. "And if I find it—"

"Perhaps we should look for it together," he said hurriedly.

A thought struck her, and her mouth went slack. "You don't trust me, do you? What, do you think I squirted whipped cream on your finger and slipped off your ring while you were dozing?"

"No," he said hotly. "But I don't expect you to be on your hands and knees—"

"You certainly expected it last night," she cut in.

His face turned purple. "What? *I'm* the one who has rug burns on my knees—"

"Well, that's what you get, Mr. Kie-yie-yippie-yie-a."

"Good morning, all."

Piper spun toward the door. To her horror, Edmund stood there with a smile plastered on his face.

"M-Mr. Blythe," she stammered.

"Piper, Mr. Bentley." He nodded at each of them in turn, then sauntered into the room as if he hadn't walked in on a shouting match.

"Edmund," Ian replied, his voice somewhat strained.

Her boss continued over to the coffee station and filled a paper cup, then added cream. "I hope you don't mind, Ian, but Piper told me this morning about her new recipe, so I thought I'd sit in on your meeting and see how you like it.''

''Mind?'' He glanced at Piper and she winced, wondering how much of their ''meeting'' Edmund had heard. ''No, I don't mind. We were just about to, um—''

*Come to blows.* ''Get started,'' Piper finished magnanimously. She yanked on the lab coat and walked over to the refrigerator, trying to get past her misery. It was useless—Ian would never give them the contract, she'd never get the bonus, she'd never have the home she wanted and she'd never have another date. *Because he has ruined me for other men.*

She removed the two new batches of sauce from the refrigerator and banged the door so hard, both men turned her way. ''Spring-loaded door,'' she lied, then moved toward the white table. Trying not to think about the consumption of the last batch she made, she put the chocolate sauce in the microwave, then removed fresh, warm chocolate muffins from the oven.

''By the way, Piper, Saint Augustine's sent us a nice thank-you letter for allowing you to chef the children's benefit dinner,'' Edmund said from the table. He winked at Ian, who pulled out a chair opposite him. ''Ms. Shepherd really knows her way around the kitchen, wouldn't you agree, Bentley?''

Feeling wicked, Ian nodded and blew into his cup of black coffee. "She fixes a nice spread, yes."

A tightening of her jaw was the only evidence that she'd heard him. He watched those wonderfully talented small hands assemble two desserts, then carry them to the table. A rich, dark aroma floated from the cakes, tickling his nose when she set the concoction before him. She pulled a fact sheet from her lab-coat pocket and lay it next to his portion.

"Gentlemen, may I present Mississippi Malted Mud Puddles."

With one look at the cake, memories of the previous night assaulted him. On cue, he began to salivate, feeling like one of Pavlov's dogs.

Edmund smiled, turning his saucer around. "Why, it's lovely, Piper. I've never seen anything like it. Have you, Bentley?"

"Er, no," he murmured. "I really can't say that I have." He glanced behind her. "Do you have any extra garnishes with the cake?"

Her blue eyes widened innocently. "Oh, I almost forgot." From behind her back, she pulled out a can of whipped cream. With an exaggerated flourish, she gave each of them a generous dollop on top of their respective cakes.

Ian stared at the fluffy cream and shifted in his seat, remembering with remarkable distinction the way she'd turned her wrist last night at the last second to put a little swirly tail on top of whatever area of his body she was covering at the time.

While he stared, a perfect-stemmed maraschino cherry plopped on top.

He looked up and she smiled back. "You do like cherries, don't you, Mr. Bentley?"

He ground his teeth to curb his burgeoning arousal. "I've been known to eat one or two."

*"Two?"* she said, her eyebrows raised. She reached into the jar she held and dropped another cherry onto his cake, flattening the whipped cream. "Perhaps you can save one to take back to Chicago with you."

She glanced to Edmund, who seemed a little frightened at her zeal for cherries. "I'll pass."

Ian pursed his lips, determined to be civil. "Aren't you going to indulge with us, Ms. Shepherd?"

Edmund laughed. "Piper's allergic to chocolate—can you believe it? A food scientist who creates some of the best desserts in the country, and she's allergic to chocolate." He scooped up a gooey bite and shoved it in his mouth, then rolled his eyes and made a contented grunt as he chewed.

Ian digested the information, then glanced up at Piper. She blushed furiously. "Allergic, you say?"

"Yeah," Edmund said thickly. "She breaks out in a rash and everything, don't you, Piper?"

She didn't answer, but rolled her shoulders as if she wanted to scratch something right then and there.

"A rash?" Ian asked, amused at this bit of news. "So, Ms. Shepherd, the occasion would have to be a rather special one before you would consume chocolate with, shall we say, *gusto?*"

Her face turned a deeper shade of pink, quite becoming with her blue eyes and blue suit and blue lab coat. "Th-there are times, understandably so, when I have to eat chocolate for the sake of my job."

"This is absolutely wonderful," Edmund exclaimed. "Do I taste coffee in this too?"

She nodded.

"Piper, my dear, you are a genius." Her boss scooped the last bite into his mouth and Ian had the feeling if he'd been alone, the man would have licked the saucer clean.

"So, tell me, Edmund," Ian said, taking another sip of his coffee. "What does your resident genius get if I contract with Blythe?"

Edmund stopped chewing, but it took a few seconds for his jowls to slow down. A slight frown creased his forehead. "Well, Bentley, I don't think—"

Ian cut him off with a casual wave. "Oh, come on, Edmund. I use bonuses and commissions to motivate my own people—I understand sales."

The older man glanced up at Piper then back to Ian. "I still don't like to discuss my employees' salaries."

"That's all right, Edmund," Piper said softly. "I don't mind if Mr. Bentley knows."

"How much?" Ian asked, locking gazes with her.

"Ten thousand," she said, her expression perfectly still.

Ian nodded, his heart squeezing with disappointment. She'd slept with him hoping he'd sign the contract and she would get the money. Well, he had to give her credit—she certainly didn't undervalue herself. "Ten grand," he repeated, stroking his chin. "I'd say that's worth a few days of itching, wouldn't you, Ms. Shepherd?"

Her eyes gave nothing away. "I'd have to say so."

Ian bit down hard on his tongue and dropped his gaze to the fact sheet. He scanned it quickly, then turned to Edmund. "Where's the contract?"

Edmund's eyes widened. "A contract? But don't you want to talk to production and marketing?"

Ian shook his head. "I know you'll work it out—I need to get back to Chicago right away." He raised his gaze to Piper. "Something there needs my immediate attention."

Edmund pulled a rolled sheath of papers from his inside coat pocket. "This is a generic agreement, but we can handle the rest of it over the ph—" He squinted his eyes at the saucer in front of Ian. "Bentley, man, you didn't even try it. I promise it's the best thing you'll ever eat—you should at least try it."

Ian signed his name on a few pages, then glanced up with a tight smile. "Trust me, Edmund, I know it's the best thing I'll ever have. Could I get copies of these, please?"

Edmund jumped up, obviously flustered. "Of course, I'll take care of it right now."

Ian stood and buttoned his jacket, avoiding her gaze. "It's been a pleasure doing business with you, Ms. Shepherd."

"And with you, Mr. Bentley," she said quietly. "I'll look for your ring, and if I find it, I'll contact your office."

He tossed a business card on the table and nodded curtly. "I hope it's insured."

She nodded back. "So do I."

"Well, goodbye then." He strode toward the door, then stopped and looked to the table where she was standing.

Her lips parted slightly, then she said, "Did you forget something?"

He simply wanted to look at her one last time. Beautiful, sensual and not nearly as naive as he had once thought. "As a matter of fact, I did." He walked back to the table slowly, wanting one last kiss. Then he remembered she didn't have a reason to play along anymore—she had the contract, and her money. Ian reached down and plucked one of the cherries from the top of his untouched dessert, and carefully wrapped it in a paper napkin that said Blythe Industries.

"To take back to Chicago with me," he said, then left.

"WHEW! Let's take a break," Granny Falkner said, dabbing at her glistening forehead.

"I wish you would take it easy," Piper said for the hundredth time since the movers had arrived.

"I'll be taking it easy for the rest of my days."

"I won't believe it until I see it." She followed her grandmother to the kitchen where they poured glasses of lemonade and sat down on the only furniture left—two step stools.

"So how are things developing between you and your Mr. Bentley?" Gran asked, sipping from her glass.

"He's not *my* Mr. Bentley," Piper corrected her. "And he went back to Chicago on Thursday."

"Oh, I see. And were you able to wow him with a chocolate dessert before he left?"

"Um-hmmm," Piper mumbled, talking into her glass. She hoped the guilty flush climbing her neck was not obvious to her grandmother's keen eyes.

"Okay, what gives?"

*Busted.* "Well," she said, twisting on the stool, "he signed the contract."

"That's wonderful," Gran said, but when Piper didn't look up, she added, "Isn't it?"

Guilt and humiliation and shame pulled at her.

"Piper, stop squirming and tell me what's bothering you."

She sat up straight, then looked her grandmother in the eye. "I think he signed the contract for the wrong reasons."

"He apparently liked the dessert. What other reason could he have had?"

Piper didn't say anything, just stared into her grandmother's eyes, begging her to understand. Suddenly, realization dawned on the older woman's face. "Oh, I see."

Squeezing the bridge of her nose with forefinger and thumb, Piper said, "I really messed up."

Ice clinked in Gran's glass. "Oh, I don't know.

Did you come up with a good idea for his restaurants?''

She nodded.

''Well, then, in a roundabout way, it seems as though everyone got what they wanted.''

Piper gave her grandmother a knowing smile. ''You're letting me off the hook.''

''Grandmother's prerogative. Besides, I don't think you messed up that badly.''

She stared into her glass, wondering why some of the lemon seeds floated and other ones sank. ''Yeah, Gran, I messed up, big time. I fell in love with him.''

Her grandmother set down her glass. ''Ah, well, that does put a different spin on things, doesn't it?''

''I suppose so.''

''At least it wasn't a meaningless encounter.''

''Not to me.''

''Did he tell you it was meaningless to him?''

''Not in so many words.''

''What words did he use exactly?''

Piper heaved a deep breath. ''It's been a pleasure doing business with you, Ms. Shepherd.''

''Oh dear.'' Her grandmother clucked. ''Well, if that's the kind of man he is, then be glad you're rid of him.''

''I suppose so,'' Piper said miserably. ''I just thought he might be the one, you know?''

"I was only teasing you the other day, my dear," her grandmother said gently. "I didn't mean to make you feel like you needed a man to be happy. You don't. I miss Nate every day that I breathe, but I'm still happy."

"I know, but I *am* getting older and all my friends are married, and I really do want the fairy tale someday—marriage to a good man, maybe even a baby."

"Someday doesn't mean it has to happen today."

"No, but…what's wrong with me, Gran?" To her horror, she burst into tears. "How could I have fallen in love with a man who doesn't love me? Is my judgment as bad as…Mom's?"

"Shush, dear," her grandmother chided gently, squeezing Piper's knee. "Your mother doesn't have bad judgment—she simply doesn't care about the consequences. That's the difference, see? You care. Besides, how do you know that Mr. Bentley doesn't love you?"

She sniffed, feeling like a teenager. "I just know."

"And does he know that you love him?"

Piper glanced up at her grandmother's wise eyes. "I don't know."

"You mean you haven't told him?"

She shook her head. "I tried to do all the things

in the book, but I messed them all up. But it says never to let a man know how you feel—at least not at first.''

Her grandmother's pale forehead wrinkled. ''What book?''

''The book you gave me last week, the one you and your sisters wrote. *The Sexton Sisters' Secret Guide*—''

*''To Marrying a Good Man,''* the older woman finished, then started laughing. ''I didn't realize I'd given you that old piece of trash.''

''Trash?'' Piper frowned. ''But you all married wonderful men.''

Gran's laughter echoed off the bare walls. ''Piper, that was fifty-odd years ago. Times have changed.''

''But not men and women.''

''Oh, yes, men and women have changed, too. For the better, I might add. I'm thrilled that you've had so many choices in your life—you got a good education, found a nice job. You don't have to get married, Piper—don't you see the beauty of it? So when you find someone you want to be with, it will be a *choice* and you'll be wonderfully happy if you wait for the right person.'' She shook her head and gripped Piper's hand. ''If you love this man, you'd better tell him.'' Then she grinned. ''And throw away that blasted book!''

Piper smiled, wanting to believe her, but she'd seen the look on Ian's face when he left—he'd even flaunted the cherry he was taking back to the woman he was going to marry. And she was half-afraid that if she called and he thought she were bothering him, he might renege on the agreement. No, she was better off not calling. Definitely.

## CHAPTER ELEVEN

*Keep in mind that some women never marry, but find gardening to be a satisfactory replacement.*

"HEY, PIPER, what's shakin'?"

Piper sat back on her heels, removed a soiled gardening glove and scratched her nose with her knuckle as Lenny walked over, carrying a cardboard box. "Just planting a few begonias, Len."

"I came to tell you goodbye."

She glanced up and shielded her eyes from the bright sun. "Goodbye?"

"I'm moving into my own place."

Piper grinned. "That's great, Len."

"Yeah," he agreed, nodding. "Got me a woman, too."

Her eyes widened. "Really?"

He looked embarrassed. "Well, she doesn't know it yet."

"Ah. Anyone I know?"

"Maybe—she's a nurse lady. Nice red hair and braces."

Piper blinked. "Janet Browning?"

"That's her," he said excitedly. "She comes to the Gas Giddyup every day for a newspaper and a Dr. Pepper."

Leaning her head to one side, Piper considered the match. It could work, she conceded. Besides, who was she to give advice on a person's love life? Ian had been gone for over a week and she still couldn't bring herself to call him. She'd finally covered the kitchen table with a quilt to keep from picturing him standing there making love to her on its surface.

"Janet's a great gal, Len. I hope it works out for you."

He nodded, then looked sheepish. "Thanks, Piper—for all your advice, I mean."

She pushed herself to her feet, brushed off her shorts and gave him a genuine smile. "No problem, Len."

"What happened to that city fella?"

Piper's pulse kicked up, the way it always did when she thought of Ian. "He went back to the city." *Back to his fiancée,* her conscience whispered. She shrugged, as if it was no big deal. As if she didn't lie awake every night on top of the covers thinking about him.

"Why didn't he take you with him?" he asked in the simple way that made sense only to Lenny.

She smiled, feeling a rush of affection for the bungling man. "Because Mudville is my home," she insisted.

"I thought you liked him," he persisted.

"I thought I did, too," she admitted. "But a relationship has to go two ways."

He frowned. "It does?"

Trying not to laugh, she nodded. "It helps."

"I'll have to remember that."

"Bye, Len." She gave him a brief hug. "Good luck."

"See ya, Piper."

She watched him walk down the sidewalk, then jump into his rattletrap car, all his worldly possessions in one box. His happy whistle floated back to her before the car roared to life and shot toward town.

The sound of her phone pealed through the open window. The Realtor, finally! She jumped the front steps two at a time, then swung open the screen door, letting it bang behind her. With her heart pounding in anticipation, she lifted the phone. "Hello?"

"Piper, this is Terri at the real-estate office."

"Did you match the offer?"

"Um, no."

"Why not?"

"Because this morning your grandmother made a counteroffer to the Warner man."

Piper gripped the phone. "But I thought he'd offered her the asking price."

"He came in just shy of it, but now Granny Falkner wants fifty thousand more."

*"What?"*

"Beats all I've ever seen," Terri declared.

Hot tears of frustration filled her eyes. "I can't touch that price."

"You'd only need to put down an additional ten thousand—twenty percent of the increase," she said hopefully. Then the woman sighed. "Of course, you could never afford the mortgage payments."

"Of course." She bit her tongue, trying to stem the tears.

"I'm sorry, Piper, but if Mr. Warner accepts your grandmother's price, she'll be sitting pretty."

"You're right." Piper sniffed, then smiled into the phone. "Of course, you're right."

"Listen, dear, I realize you've got your heart set on your gran's place, but there are lots of darling little houses you can easily afford, and then you wouldn't be strapped for cash."

"I'll let you know, Terri. Thanks."

"Sure thing. Oh, and call me back if you happen to win the lottery."

Piper smirked, then hung up, feeling elated for her grandmother—if she had to see her home turned into a hotel, she was going to force Mr. Warner to make it worth her while—but she felt heartbroken for herself.

Heartbroken.

She stared at the phone for a long while, imagining where Ian might be at this time on a Saturday. Working? At the club? Having lunch? On his honeymoon? She slid open the junk drawer by the phone where she'd stuck his business card and ran her fingers over the raised letters. "I love you," she whispered, then frowned. "I think."

The washing machine buzzed, so she dropped the card back into the drawer and padded to the louvered closet that housed her washer and dryer. With lots of sunshine left in the day, she decided to hang her sheets on the line. With a start, she realized they were the same ones she and Ian had lain under—she remembered how his muscular arm had looked against the floral pattern. Oh, well, she would forget that detail someday, when the sheets were relegated to the giveaway bin or the ragbag.

She carried the basket of linens out the back door and hung the sheets first, then the pillowcases, on a cotton cord strung between two metal poles. When she snapped the last pillowcase to take out the wrinkles, a small, lumpy object flew up in the air, then thumped on the ground, glinting in the sun. *The ring.* With her heart pounding, she plucked it from the grass, surprised at its weight, dazzled by the size of the stones. Blatantly masculine, the thick band of gold was slightly rounded on the inside— the sign of a good ring, she supposed, although she had no way of knowing. Two rows of diamonds paraded around one half of the ring's perimeter, each of them larger than the diamond stud earrings on which she'd splurged two years ago. One offending prong poked sideways—the one that had stuck her, she presumed.

She tested the weight of the ring in her hand and wondered how much it was worth. Ten thousand? Twenty? She shook her head ruefully, thinking of the things she could do with that kind of money. Then she stopped and curled her fingers over the ring. *The things she could do with that kind of money.* There was a pawnshop in Tupelo... No, she couldn't. She wouldn't.

*But it's probably insured,* a dark voice inside her whispered. *Ian will simply get another.* And some tiny part of her marveled at the irony of her pawning the proposed wedding ring of the man she loved.

While the larger, saner part of her considered the sentence for insurance fraud.

Piper sighed and crushed the ring in her hand

until her flesh hurt. Then before she could change her mind or do something hokey like write out a script, she marched into the house and dialed his office number in Chicago. With each ring, she grew more nervous, hoping he would answer, praying he wouldn't. Finally, the phone bounced over to a voice-mail recorder and his voice came over the line.

"Hello, this is Ian Bentley of the Bentley Group. I'll be on vacation until Monday the sixth of July. Leave a message and I'll call you back."

While the message went on to give directions for how to reach other members of his staff if this call was an emergency, Piper's mind raced. Today was June 13, so he'd be out for the next three weeks…and she couldn't imagine the infamous workaholic Ian Bentley taking time off to do anything short of… Her heart sank and her knees buckled. He *had* gotten married. She hung up.

"FIFTY THOUSAND?" Ian asked, surprised. "She didn't seem like a shyster to me, Ben—she just seemed like a nice old lady. Sort of grandmotherly, actually."

"Well, she's a savvy grandmother," Ben barked. "What do you think? You saw the place. Is it worth it?"

"To me? Sure," Ian said. "Ben, her old man built the place himself."

"And?"

"*And?* He completed the inside finishing work with wooden nails, man."

"And?"

"*And* it's an unbelievable place. It's got character and warmth and...the lady even caned the seats of the rocking chairs sitting on the front porch."

"Oh, that's nice," Ben said pleasantly, then he growled, "Maybe that's why she raised the price fifty thousand dollars—she's throwing in the chairs!"

"As a matter of fact, Mrs. Falkner told me she was moving to a much smaller place, so maybe she will sell some of her furniture. There was a man's mahogany wardrobe in the second spare bedroom that I'd love to—"

"Ian," Ben broke in. "What's with you? I'm talking business, you're talking Walton's Mountain."

Dropping into his father's chair in the library, Ian leaned his head back and laughed. "Sorry, pal. I guess being home with my folks is making me sentimental."

"Yeah, well, don't start blubbering on me. Tell Mr. and Mrs. B. hello for me, would you?"

"Sure, Ben." Ian leaned forward, resting his elbows on his knees. "And keep me posted on the Falkner house, would you?"

"Good night, John-Boy."

Smiling, Ian hung up the phone, then steepled his hands together over his stomach.

"Was that Meredith?" Fresh from a game of golf, his mom walked in and drew a glass of water from the wet bar.

"Uh, no, that was Ben. He said to say hello."

She drank, nodding.

"Mom." Ian stood and turned his back to her, in case his expression gave away too much.

"Who is she, Ian?"

He faced her, frowning sourly. "How do you do that?"

"You mean, how do I know you've met someone?" She held up her fingers and bent them back dramatically as she spoke. "First, you call and tell me you're taking a vacation. *Then* you tell me it's a three-week vacation. *Then* you tell me you're coming to see me and your father. *Then* you come alone." She stopped, sat down in a nearby chair, and smiled. "Is that enough or should I mention how moony you've been?"

He scoffed. "Moony?"

"So, what's her name, and does Meredith know?"

After a deep breath, he surrendered. "Piper Shepherd and yes. Meredith proposed to me a couple of weeks ago. I declined when I came back from a business trip to Mississippi."

She crossed her arms. "I can't blame Meredith, she's waited longer than I would have."

He smirked. "I know, I shouldn't have let it drift on for so long."

"So you've drifted on to someone else, someone in Mississippi?"

Feeling like a schoolboy, he nodded. "Maybe."

"Maybe?"

He shrugged. "I don't know how she feels about me."

"Did you ask her?"

He pursed his lips. "No."

She groaned and sat up in her chair. "What *is* it with your generation? You think everyone around you is psychic or something." Rising to her feet, she smiled and gentled her voice. "Call her, son. Why should you go another day not knowing?" She kissed him on the cheek and walked out, gesturing pointedly to the phone as she left.

Ian lifted the handset and stared until it blurred into two. Why, indeed? How could he explain that while their night together had been an emotional upheaval for him, the incident had been but a business ploy for Piper? And that he was afraid the feelings he had for Piper were out of some perverse relief that their interlude had kept him from making a mistake by marrying Meredith.

He set down the phone. No, he would not call her and leave himself hanging in the wind until he had things straight in his head. He needed some distance from the whole Meredith thing, and the whole Piper thing. After his vacation, he might give her a call. Maybe. Perhaps.

"WHAT'S YOUR SCHEDULE like for next weekend?" Justine asked breathlessly over the telephone.

"Hello to you, too," Piper said, wrestling with a roll of clear packing tape. So far, more of it had landed on her legs and feet than on the box she was trying to wrap.

"I'm serious—are you free next Saturday?"

"Well, I'll have to cancel my weekend getaway with the two Chippendale dancers, but for you— hey, I'd do it. What's up?"

"I'm pregnant."

Piper dropped the tape and watched it roll away, knowing she'd probably never find the end again. "Justine, you're joking, right?"

"Nope. I'm going to be a mommy!" She screamed with happiness. "I'm four months."

"That's unbelievable! Four months?" Piper calculated ahead to the wedding date two months away. "That dress will be a little tight, won't it, Jus?"

"That's why we're getting married on Saturday!" she sang. "At three o'clock!"

Piper blinked. "You're going to have a sit-down dinner for four hundred people this Saturday?"

"No, silly, we're having to scale back a little—we're on a budget now, you know. Just a small ceremony, family and close friends. You'll still be my maid of honor, won't you?"

"Of course I will! But the dresses couldn't possibly be ready, could they?" She crossed her fingers and looked heavenward.

"Oh, don't worry, they'll be finished. Mother said we might have to tape the hems, but they'll be ready."

Piper wrinkled her nose. "Hair bows, too?"

"Hair bows, too… Hey, you had to hang up when I called for your measurements before you could tell me how your manhunt is going." She giggled, giddy from hormones, Piper guessed.

"Manhunt?" she parroted, then sighed. "I'm going to see if Rich wants to come to the wedding with me."

"No luck, huh? And Rich is still teetering on the fence?"

Piper frowned. "Cut him some slack, Justine.

Rich is a great guy. Are you getting married in the same church?"

"Yep."

"What time should I be there?"

"The ceremony starts at three o'clock, but the pictures are at two, so come early and we'll get dressed together."

"I'll be there," she promised. "Congratulations!"

She hung up the phone, smiling, happier than she'd been in the longest time. Even when she looked at the package containing the ring she was mailing back to Ian, the hurt had dulled to a bittersweet ache. She'd be all right in a few months, she decided. And maybe she'd even embark on another manhunt—except this time with a better laid plan.

She found a box of plain stationery to write him a note. "Dear Ian," she read as she wrote. No. "Dear Mr. Bentley." Much better. "I found the ring you were looking for in my laundry—" She bit her bottom lip. "I found the ring you were looking for, period. Have a nice day." She made a face. "Have a nice married life." She drew a line through it. "Say hello to your cherry." She scratched out that phrase, too, but it made her laugh. "I love you." *This* she drew a line through, and didn't laugh. "Sincerely, Piper Shepherd."

She recopied the keeper phrases in neat script,

and folded the paper. Resisting the ridiculous urge to kiss it, she went in search of more tape. After she inserted the note, she wrapped up the package so that it was completely watertight, just in case the delivery truck rode into a canal or something. She drove past the post office, telling herself that the courier in Tyson would be faster, while admitting to herself she was in no hurry—as soon as the package left her possession, all direct ties to Ian would be lost.

Feeling like a criminal, she sat in her van for forty minutes, until just before the place closed. Then she filled out a neat mailing label from his business card and watched as the man tossed the ring on a heap of other packages that were being loaded. Soon it disappeared from sight, and Piper drove home, hitting downtown Mudville during prime cruising hour.

She saw Gary Purdue and his girlfriend had gotten back together. Lenny and Janet pulled up beside her in his belch-mobile, and to her amazement they seemed to be having a good time. "There's someone for everyone," she muttered, shaking her head, then frowning in the side mirror. "Except me."

When she arrived home with a chicken sandwich, she decided it was almost too hot to eat. She turned up the fan on the counter, its intensity kicking up bits of tape and paper from her packing job. She dragged a small can behind her as she collected the garbage. When her fingers closed around a piece of folded stationery, she frowned, then remembered her scratch note. Laughing at her own antics on paper, she unfolded the note...then nearly had a stroke.

In her spasmodic hands, she held the nice note, the pretty note...the edited note. And her silly, catty and—she gulped—*honest* note was somewhere in the mail, hurtling toward his office. She clawed her way to the phone and called the package company, letting it ring one hundred and two times before giving up. Then, admitting defeat, she turned off all the lights, curled into a ball on her bed and cried herself to sleep.


AMUSED, Ian tried his best not to laugh. "She raised it by another twenty-five thousand?"

"Yes, can you believe it? I was being a nice guy and met her halfway on her last price hike, and then she jacks the price up even further! Are you sure this woman is stable, Ian?"

He wet his lips, rarely having seen Ben bested. "She seemed stable to me."

"Well, I think she's a lunatic!" he thundered. "I'm going to meet her halfway on this offer and she's not getting a penny more!" He slammed down the phone.

Ian sat and listened to the ringer fade. "And that'll show her, Ben," he murmured.

Then he dialed his voice mail and jotted down a few names and numbers. He hadn't stopped hoping that Piper had found the silly ring and would call him. Meredith hadn't insured the ring yet, so he simply had the purchase price transferred from her charge card to his. He hadn't offered an explanation for the ring's disappearance, and she hadn't asked for one.

He listened to the last message, but could barely concentrate on the words of a West Coast associate. Saving it for later, Ian hung up, realizing he had undergone a subtle change in the last few days. Thoughts of Piper still plagued him every waking minute, but now he realized he wasn't as anxious for those thoughts to be gone. When had he stopped fighting the fact that he loved her? Before he could change his mind, Ian dialed directory assistance.

"What city?"

"Mudville, Mississippi."

"What listing?"

"Falkner, Mrs. Ellen Falkner."

"That phone has been forwarded to a new number. I can connect you."

The phone rang three times before she answered. "Hello?"

"Mrs. Falkner, you might not remember me. My name is Ian Bentley."

"I certainly do remember you. How can I help you, Mr. Bentley?"

"I'll be coming to Mudville next week and I was hoping I could stop by and talk to you about the house."

"Certainly. Are you coming back for business or pleasure?"

He smiled wryly. "Pleasure, I hope, although I won't know until I get there."

"Call anytime—I'll meet you at the house."

"Oh, and Mrs. Falkner, I know this is asking a lot, but could you hold off on accepting any offers on the house?"

"But your associate is the only interested buyer, Mr. Bentley."

"I know," he admitted sheepishly. "Can you stall him?"

"Mr. Bentley." Her voice was rich with suggestion. "Are you suggesting that I jerk Mr. Warner around?"

He laughed. "Don't worry—Ben can handle it."

"Tell me, are you yourself interested in purchasing the house?"

"Maybe."

"For commercial purposes?"

"No," he said firmly. "I can't give you any

guarantees about buying it, because it depends on...someone else.'' He swallowed. ''But if I buy your house, Mrs. Falkner, I plan to live there.''

''Such a big house for one person, Mr. Bentley—and I should know.''

''That's the someone I was talking about, Mrs. Falkner. If she says yes, then I'll be making an offer on your home.''

''Oh, that sounds wonderful,'' she declared. ''There haven't been any children in the house for a long, long time. Mr. Bentley, if your young lady says yes, will you bring her by so I can meet her?''

''Sure thing, Mrs. Falkner. I'll call you. Goodbye.''

He put the phone down and stood up, unsure of where to start. ''Mom,'' he called as she walked by the library, ''I have to leave tomorrow morning.''

She frowned. ''Well, you don't have to look so happy about it.''

''I'm going to Mississippi.''

Her eyes lit up. ''Did you call your Ms. Shepherd?''

''No, I have to go back to Chicago first to tie up some loose ends at the office, but after that, I'm going to see her.''

Her smiled wavered. ''You're just going to drop in?''

''You don't think that's a good idea?''

"Well…"

"You're right," he said with a sigh. Ian glanced at his watch. "Friday afternoon at four o'clock—she's probably still at the office." Without a word, his mother slipped from the room and closed the French doors, giving him a wink through the glass before she turned and walked away.

Ian dialed directory assistance again, then wrote down the number for Blythe Industries. After a deep breath, he punched in the number, identified himself and asked for Piper, his heart beating as loudly and crazily as a child's drum.

"I'm sorry, Mr. Bentley, but Ms. Shepherd is out today," the receptionist said. "Oh, hold on, please. Mr. Blythe was walking by and he'd like a word with you."

"Bentley?" Edmund's gravelly voice came over the line. "Is there something I can help you with?"

"Uh, no, Edmund." Ian suppressed his disappointment. "I…I wanted a word with Ms. Shepherd, that's all."

"They'll be back in the office early next week," Edmund said cheerfully.

Frowning, Ian asked, "They?"

"Rich and Piper—wedding in Tupelo, tomorrow. They have friends who live there so they asked for a few extra days off."

His heart stopped. "Wedding?" His throat convulsed as he remembered her words. *My ideal wedding would be to leave town quietly then come back married.* "Do you know where or what time?" he gasped.

"They didn't talk to me about it," Edmund said, then laughed. "Why?"

Ian grasped for an explanation. "I, uh, I have business there and I thought I might try to catch up with her, er, them." Knowing he sounded insane, he squeezed the bridge of his nose between forefinger and thumb.

Mr. Blythe's tone sounded rich with innuendo. "I thought you and Piper hit it off, Bentley. So I can't blame you for not wanting to wait until she gets back. Hang on."

Ian heard the man asking the receptionist if she had details of the wedding. His mind raced—he'd lost her. Tomorrow she was marrying another man.

"You're in luck," Edmund boomed. "Sheila doesn't know where they're staying, but the wedding is at the Saint Stephen's Catholic Church on Pascoe Road at three o'clock."

"Thanks, Edmund." His head pounded as he hung up the phone. He scrubbed both hands over his face and sighed. One thing was certain—tying up loose ends at the office would have to wait. The start-up venture of his life waited in Tupelo, Mississippi.

# CHAPTER TWELVE

*And finally, remember it's bad luck to cry on your wedding day.*

"MY GOODNESS, Piper, why the devil are you crying? I'm the one with the hormones—I should be upset that the record for daily rainfall was set on my wedding day." Dressed in full bridal regalia, Justine leaned forward and offered Piper a tissue. "Come on, out with it."

Piper blew her nose, then sniffed mightily. "You don't want to hear about it."

Justine checked her watch. "We have ten minutes before the music starts, and we're both dressed. So talk."

She welled up again, and Justine clucked.

"Don't cry—talk. You're scaring me."

"It's just a m-man."

"Surprise, surprise."

"You knew?"

"Piper, give me some credit, okay? Is he a local guy?"

She sniffed. "No. He's from Chicago and he does business with the company I work for."

"What's his name?"

Piper hiccuped. "Ian Bentley. And he's married."

Justine's eyes bugged. "Married? Geez, Piper, I thought you knew better."

She shook her head, and watched in the mirror as the big salmon-colored satin bow in her hair flapped like a butterfly. "No, he wasn't married when I—when we—oh, God, I feel like such a *fool*."

"Well, if he wasn't married—"

"He got married as soon as he went back to Chicago." Her chin quivered.

"Piper," her friend said, touching her hand. "If the man met you, then married someone else, *he's* the fool."

"Wait until you've heard the rest of the story."

"What? Tell me!"

"He sort of…lost the engagement ring his fiancée had given him…in my bed."

Justine pursed her pink lips and bobbed her head. "Okay—there's a movie."

"Well, first I didn't believe that he'd actually lost the ring, but then I found it about a week later, and by that time he'd already gone on his honeymoon."

"So you hocked it, I hope."

She shook her head. "The thing was worth a freaking fortune—I was afraid I'd get hard labor."

"So what did you do?"

"I mailed it back to him."

"You *mailed* back a ring that was worth too much money to be pawned?"

Piper frowned. "I called a jeweler and he said it was the safest way."

"Okay, okay, you mailed the ring, end of story."

"No. Because when I wrapped up the ring, I wanted to put a note inside."

Justine dabbed at Piper's eye makeup. "Something nasty, I hope."

"Well, the practice note *was* a little spiteful and not very nice."

"And?"

"And I put in the practice note by mistake and mailed it."

Her friend's eyes widened. "And *this* is why you're crying? Because you sent a jerky note to a jerky guy? Geez, the man should send you a car or something for sending that ring back to him and getting him out of the crapper with his girlfriend."

"Wife," she corrected.

"Whatever."

"But that's not the worst part."

"Oh, so there *is* a worst part?"

"On the practice note, I sort of wrote 'I love you.'"

Justine made a painful face. "Are you sure? Think—because if you drew a little eyeball with the lashes around it, and a heart and a sheep, men don't get it. It's a code they can't break."

"Justine, I spelled it out. I...love...you. No pictures, no codes."

"Oh, geez, Piper, what were you thinking?"

A tear slipped down her cheek. "I was thinking that I loved him." She fell against her friend, sobbing.

Justine rubbed her back. "There, there, men are pigs. Just think, you'll probably live twenty years longer than he will."

A knock on the door sounded. "That's our cue, sweetie," her friend declared.

Piper drew up, dried up and stood up. "I'm sorry, Justine. This is the happiest day of your life, and I've been pouring out my pathetic little tragedy."

"Hey, that's what friends are for," the other woman assured her.

"Let's go get you married," Piper said, smiling wide.

Another knock sounded, this one louder.

"The bride is on her way," Piper said loudly.

"Piper, it's me—Ian."

Piper stopped, paralyzed. Justine gasped and whispered. "Is that him?"

Her heart beating wildly, Piper nodded, her eyes wide.

"Piper, talk to me," he said through the door.

She cleared her throat. "What are you doing here?"

"I came to talk you out of making a big mistake."

"What mistake is that?" she asked, confused.

"Marrying Rich—don't do it."

She and Justine exchanged puzzled glances.

"What the hell is he talking about?" Justine hissed.

Piper shrugged.

"Play along," her friend encouraged, nudging her.

Moving closer to the door, Piper swallowed. "W-why not marry Rich? Are you so disenchanted with marriage already, Ian, that you don't want anyone else to be happy?"

"I didn't marry her, Piper." His voice reverberated, low but clear.

Her heart skyrocketed. Justine grabbed her arm and made a squeaky noise. Piper tried to keep her voice steady when she asked, "Why didn't you marry her?"

She heard a fumbling noise and a scraping sound

at her feet. When she looked down, a folded napkin lay by the toe of her salmon-colored shoe. She bent to retrieve it and unfolded it slowly, recognizing the name of her company printed across the paper, uncovering a reddish stain. At last she revealed a stemmed maraschino cherry, and tears filled her eyes.

"I love you, Piper. Please don't marry him until we've had a chance to talk."

"This is great!" Justine whispered. "Open the door, for heaven's sake."

Piper nodded numbly, but her hands wouldn't move. "I can't."

Justine unlocked the door with the flick of her wrist, then pulled open the door. Ian stood in the doorway, one arm on either side. Soaked to the skin, his dark hair hung in his eyes, while water dripped off the sleeves of his black suit. He stared in confusion first at Justine, then at Piper as he took in their respective garb.

"Piper—"

"I told you," she cut in, trying to keep her voice breezy. "Always a bridesmaid."

He straightened, his forehead wrinkling. "But I...I mean, you and Rich...and then Edmund..." He gestured aimlessly, his face reddening.

Fingering the cherry, she smiled, telling herself

not to get her hopes too high. "Rich and I are not getting married. We've never even dated."

He lifted his hands in the air, then jammed them on his hips. "I feel like an idiot."

Piper studied the tips of her shoes. "So you want to take it all back?"

Ian was silent so long, she finally lifted her gaze, afraid of what she'd see in his eyes. He reached for her, crushing her against him. "Not on your life," he breathed before he captured her lips in an urgent kiss.

When he released her, she lifted the cherry to his mouth and pulled out the stem as he clasped the red fruit between white teeth. He slowly chewed and swallowed, then kissed her, sharing the sweetness. Finally he raised his head and laughed. "Hey, what about you?"

"Me?"

"*I* made a complete fool of myself to prove how much I love you. So, what about you?"

Piper ran a tongue over her tingling lips. "I guess that means you haven't received the package."

"What package?"

"Your engagement ring. I found it and sent it to your office."

He shook his head. "I've been visiting my folks, then I came straight here when I heard that—" Ian stopped and grinned sheepishly. "Well, when I *thought* I heard that you were getting married."

She grinned.

"So," he continued with a mischievous expression. "Are you saying that because you returned the ring I'm supposed to believe you're madly in love with me?"

Embarrassment flooded her. "Um, no, there's the matter of a note," she murmured, looping her arms around his neck.

"A note?" he asked, nuzzling her ear.

"We'll talk about it later," she said, rolling her shoulders in pure happiness. "For now, you'll have to take my word for it that I love you."

"Marry me, Piper." His dark eyes shone. A drop of rain trailed off the tip of his nose. His lips parted expectantly.

Piper trembled with desire, love and anticipation of their life together. "Yes, Ian, I'll marry you." He whooped and kissed her hard, his tongue seeking, his breath ragged. They parted at the sound of Justine clearing her throat behind them. Piper laughed—she'd nearly forgotten about her friend.

"Nice day for a wedding," Justine said, smiling.

She and Ian stared at each other, eyebrows high. "Why not?" he finally asked.

"We could have a double wedding," Justine said, squeezing Piper's shoulders. "Most of our sorority sisters are here.'' Her friend lowered her voice. ''Girl, when you go on a manhunt, you get serious.''

Everything was moving so fast. ''B-but you're all wet,'' Piper said to Ian, surveying his suit.

''Sort of like when I first met you,'' he declared, dishing up a devilishly happy expression.

''Sort of,'' she admitted, her head spinning. ''But my dress...'' She glanced down at the salmon-colored bedspread she wore.

''Don't worry about your dress,'' he teased, leaning close. ''I'll have you out of it in no time.''

Justine picked up her bridal bouquet, divided it and pressed half the flowers into Piper's hand. ''I'll let the director know there's been a change of plans,'' Justine offered, lifting her skirt and bustling from the room.

''But where will we live?'' Piper asked, troubled at the thought of leaving her grandmother, of leaving her job, despite the fact that she loved Ian very much.

''In Mudville,'' he said. ''There's a woman there who can vouch for my good intentions.''

She withdrew a single white lily from her make-shift bouquet, inserted it through the buttonhole in his lapel, then frowned. ''What woman?''

His eyes grew warm as he settled his arms around her waist. ''Relax, sweetheart, I think you're going to like this lady. She's certainly anxious to meet you. And wait until you see this incredible house…''

If you liked *Manhunting in Mississippi*, by Stephanie Bond, you'll love the feature recipe, Mississippi Malted Mud Puddles. This marvelous marbleized dessert is guaranteed to satisfy the most ardent chocolate lover's appetite. Make Mississippi Malted Mud Puddles tonight and share them with someone you love!

### Mississippi Malted Mud Puddles

**Cake:**

Cream together in a medium mixing bowl:

> ⅓ cup margarine
> 1 egg
> ½ cup white granulated sugar
> ½ tsp vanilla extract

In a separate bowl, sift together:

> ¼ cup cocoa
> 1 cup self-rising flour
> 1 cup chocolate-flavored dry malted milk

Add dry ingredients to wet, alternately with:

³/₄ cup prepared coffee (leftover coffee is fine; the stronger the coffee, the more intense the chocolate flavor)

Stir by hand until ingredients are just mixed. Pour batter into well-greased loaf pan or muffin pan (fill cups to halfway level; makes 10-12 regular-size muffins). Bake at 350°F for 25 to 35 minutes until toothpick inserted in the middle comes out clean. Be careful not to overbake.

While the batter bakes, prepare the sauces, one to serve cold, the other warm:

**Malted Chocolate Sauce** (serve chilled)

Add ¹/₃ cup whipped cream to ³/₄ cup chocolate-flavored malted milk; mix by hand or electric mixer until the sauce is fluffy, but pourable. Refrigerate.

**Dark Chocolate Sauce** (serve warm)

In a medium saucepan, combine over low heat (don't bring to a boil) until warm and smooth:

¹/₄ cup margarine
¹/₂ cup cocoa
³/₄ cup white granulated sugar
¹/₃ cup prepared coffee
1 tsp vanilla extract

Serve cake warm from the oven in bowls, top with cold malted chocolate sauce and warm dark chocolate sauce. Garnish with whipped cream and a stemmed cherry if desired. Enjoy!

# WRAPPED AND READY

## Julie Kenner

# CHAPTER ONE

ANNIE SILVER SMOOTHED the skirt of her super-short elf costume, wondering if perhaps she should have changed before the annual holiday party for the staff of Carrington's Department Store. Except for two other elves and Santa, everyone else wore typical workday attire.

And although Annie had been perfectly comfortable guiding children to Santa's lap or working the gift-wrap table, now she felt decidedly out of place.

She was pondering the possibility of sneaking off to raid the women's casual wear department when Faith flounced over, looking gorgeous as usual in a loose red dress that cinched at the waist. In one easy movement, she handed Annie a fresh glass of wine and leaned in close. "It's not easy being green," she whispered, then burst into peals of laughter.

"Thanks." Annie flashed her friend a wry glance. "You're making me feel so much better. I'm standing out like a sore thumb, and people are staring."

"No, Paul's the sore thumb, since he's Santa and all in red. You can have a green thumb. Except there aren't any plants around."

Annie couldn't help it; she laughed. "Whatever. They're staring."

"So what? You look hot. Green, but hot. And isn't that what you wanted?"

"I suppose." As she had every year since high school, she'd signed on as a temporary holiday employee because she absolutely adored everything about the Christmas season. This year, though, she was interested in one particular fringe benefit that came with the job—Brent Carrington. He'd never once noticed Annie. Not through four years of high school, not when she'd worked summers during college in his family's department store, and certainly never at the annual holiday party. This year, Annie hoped that would change.

Faith downed the last of her wine, then smirked. "Oh, please. Could you be more nonchalant? You've been planning this for months. You want him." She stepped back, her assessing gaze skimming up Annie's body. "And I'd say tonight you've got the goods to get him."

"I hope you're right," Annie said, even as her gaze scanned the guests, hoping for a glimpse of the man in question. Come January, Annie was leaving her hometown of Bishop, Ohio, for the Big

Apple. But before she left, she intended to give herself the one thing she'd always wanted but couldn't have—Brent Carrington.

They may have grown up in the same town, but they had never lived in the same world. That was a simple fact of life. Brent was a *Carrington*—pronounced with nose in the sky and much pomp and circumstance. Annie's dad drove a truck and her mom waited tables. Their name might be Silver, but their lifestyle sure wasn't.

"I can't believe I'm doing this," Annie said.

"I can." Faith squeezed her hand, and Annie gratefully squeezed back, accepting some of her friend's innate strength. "You played by the rules your whole life and it didn't get you anywhere. Good little Annie who nobody even noticed. And now you've finally grown up and decided to go after what you want. It worked for that job in New York, and it'll work for Brent Carrington, too."

Annie pulled in a deep breath, hoping Faith was right. She'd always been the good, quiet student. Straight A's. Doing exactly what the teacher said. No cutting corners. No taking wild risks. She hadn't even signed up for a pottery class because she was afraid that the grading was too subjective. And if she got a B—or, heaven forbid, a C—she'd lose her chance at a much-needed scholarship.

But while she might have been an academic success, elsewhere, she was a complete failure. Assertiveness had never been her forte, and she'd spent most of her youth on the sidelines. Mentally, she lifted her chin. Maybe the old Annie did, but not the new Annie. The new Annie had been gutsy enough to fly to New York, knock on doors, and wait in reception areas to get the interviews she wanted—and the ploy had worked.

She only hoped her ploy to get a single, passion-filled night with the one man she'd ever wanted would work as well.

A waiter passed by, and Faith grabbed a stuffed mushroom, then gestured across the room with it before popping it in her mouth. "Tha's him."

"What?"

Faith swallowed. "Over there. By Santa's Village. Brent's here."

Annie sucked in a breath, a warm flush enveloping her entire body just from the thought of seeing Brent again. She was almost afraid to turn and actually look at him, for fear she'd melt right into the floor.

"Go on!" Faith gave her a little push on the shoulder.

"I don't think I can." At the moment, she was having trouble even forcing words past her lips.

Faith rolled her eyes. "Forget nerves. This is your last chance. Brent's the only guy I've ever known you to be truly hot for. You want this, and you deserve it. A last fling before you fly off into the sunset.'' She grinned. ''So go get him, girl.''

Faith was right; she did want this. She wanted Brent. ''Wish me luck.''

''Luck.''

Trying to keep her breathing under control, she turned until she was facing Santa's Village. She didn't see him, and battled a wave of fear that he'd turned and left after Faith had spotted him. ''Where is—?''

And then there he was. The words caught in her throat, and she closed her mouth. He'd moved to a far wall, secluded from most of the revelers, and was leaning casually against it. As she worked up her courage to approach, she let her gaze skim over him, taking in his lean physique and broad shoulders.

The Carringtons had always been the royalty of Bishop, and Brent's classic features certainly fit that bill. A perfect jawline, now sporting a five o'clock shadow, and ears she longed to trace with her fingertip. Even his hair was perfect—dark brown and in place, except for one unruly bit that hung on to his forehead, as if telling the world that despite his breeding, Brent Carrington had a wild side, too.

But it was his eyes that had always intrigued her. Deep blue, like the ocean. Eyes that could look into a woman's heart and tell exactly what she needed. He'd never once turned those eyes on her. Tonight, though, Annie intended to make Brent look at her— and really see her.

Gathering her courage, she approached, hoping against hope that he would at least remember her. She moved closer, imagining that they'd come to the party together, and that he'd signaled for her to return to his side.

Stopping in front of him, she looked up, smiling tentatively. "Hi, Brent." She'd hoped for a husky, sexy voice, but the words came out in a squeak.

At first, his face registered confusion, and she fought a flash of panic. But then his eyes cleared, and he moved toward her so he was no longer leaning against the wall.

"Annie Silver," he said, the corner of his perfect mouth pulling up into a smile. "You look fabulous."

"I'm glad you think so," she said, mentally crossing her fingers. Then, fortified by the several glasses of wine she'd downed over the last two hours, she pressed on. "Because I have a little something in mind for tonight."

"Oh?" So far, he hadn't bolted. Score one for her team. "What's that?"

"An early Christmas present to myself, actually.'' She sucked in a deep breath. *Now or never,* she thought, drawing courage from the hint of interest she saw reflected in his eyes. ''What I want in my stocking is *you.*''

## CHAPTER TWO

"EXCUSE ME?" Brent's body tightened as Annie's lips curved around the word *you.* "I'm your present?" That couldn't be what she meant. Today simply wasn't his lucky day.

But she was nodding, and damned if his groin wasn't tightening in response. Which meant that Brent's day—hell, his entire week—was suddenly looking up.

"You heard me," she whispered.

He'd heard her, alright. Hell, every fiber in his body had heard her—and reacted accordingly. He just hadn't believed his ears. But if he'd heard right, Annie Silver actually wanted him in her bed. Considering the sultry expression in her pale gray eyes and the flush on her cheeks, he was sure he'd nailed the situation.

The only question that remained was *why?* Not that he was stupid enough to put a hold on the situation by asking.

"I...I'm sorry," she stammered, and he realized

he hadn't answered aloud. "This was stupid. I should go—"

"No." The word burst from him. Reaching out, he grazed his fingers over her bare arm, delighting in the little moan that escaped her lips. "You can't say something like that to a man and then leave."

"Too impolite?" A smile touched her mouth, and he was glad to see she'd relaxed just a bit. Good. He didn't know what was going on in her head, but if the evening was going to lead where he hoped, he wanted her relaxed.

"We all have to live by the rules of polite society."

"What if I don't feel like being polite?" she asked, moving closer still until he could feel her heat.

"Sweetheart, that's all right with me." His body tightened, and his erection pressed painfully against the confines of his slacks. He fought not to grab her around the waist and pull her close. They were somewhat secluded behind Santa's Village, but they were hardly alone.

"It is?" Surprise laced her voice, and once again he was struck by the dichotomy between the boldness of her actions and the hesitancy in her eyes.

"Come on." More roughly than he intended, he took her hand, leading her toward the elevator. He needed to get away from prying eyes and questioning glances.

He wanted what she wanted—no question about that. But he didn't intend to take it until he understood her motives. He didn't know if that made him chivalrous or self-indulgent, and he didn't care. Just now he wanted to get to the bottom of this. Because only then could he lose himself inside her. And that, frankly, was one damned strong motivating factor.

She followed in silence until they stopped, waiting for the elevator to appear. "Where are we going?"

"Someplace quiet." He had no idea where, though. The store was filled with employees. Not one square inch would provide any privacy.

"Brent!" His father's voice underscored the point. "There you are."

Trying for nonchalance, his lips curved in greeting. "Father." He nodded toward Annie. "You remember Annie Silver."

"Of course," he said pleasantly. But the tightness in his father's face indicated another emotion. Winston Carrington III might be polite, but he was also a snob.

"Nice to see you, Mr. Carrington," Annie said. "And, uh, it was great bumping into you, Brent." She took a step away, and Brent realized her nerve was fading again. "I…uh…should go find Faith."

No way was he letting her get away. In one fluid motion he reached for her elbow, urging her back toward him. "I thought you promised to help me." He smiled at his father. "The champagne's running low. I'm going to go see how much we have left."

"Excellent." Winston gave him a hearty slap on the back, even while he frowned in Annie's direction. "I'll see you later, son. And tomorrow I want you managing the toy department."

"I know, Father," he said flatly. The last thing he wanted was to spend his Saturday within fifteen feet of Santa's Village and all the Christmas hokeyness his father had crammed into the store.

Then again, Annie would be there, so that would take some of the edge off the punishment. He cast a quick glance her way, taking in the so-short elf costume and green tights. The outfit hugged her curves, leaving nothing to the imagination, while at the same time managing to seem tame. Her hair hung down to her shoulders in a mass of curls that he supposed destroyed the elfin image somewhat. But he was happy for the trade, especially since he intended to lose himself in those soft brown waves.

The elevator arrived, and Brent ushered Annie on, then pushed the down button. He'd helped the caterers carry the last case of champagne up from the basement two hours ago, so he knew no one would disturb them.

As they entered the darkened room, he turned away from her to lock the door behind him. In that brief moment, she scampered away, ending up underneath the one low window that backed the alley.

The moonlight filtered in through the wire mesh, setting her skin to glow. Especially in her costume, she looked ethereal, beautiful. He was hard as a rock just from looking at her. Now he wanted to touch her...stroke her soft skin...tease her nipples....

"I'm sorry," she said, her eyes meeting his. He saw regret reflected there. Regret and uncertainty, but also a bit of pride. In one fluid motion, she pulled herself up and headed for the door. If she went through it, he wouldn't stop her. Her seductive words and glances had brought him to his knees, and he had no idea what her game was, but there was no way in hell he'd ever force a woman.

She dragged her teeth across her lower lip. "I was being silly." She shook her head as her fingers flipped the deadbolt. "I should never have—"

Abruptly she quieted, her eyes wide as she turned to stare at him. "It won't open."

In an instant, he was by her side, her nearness disconcerting even as he focused on the door. "The time lock," he said, the words coming out in a rush as memory returned. "Father installed a time lock. Part of the new security system."

She sagged against the door. "When..."

"The morning. Seven, I think."

"Oh." Her lips formed a perfect circle, encasing the single small sound.

"Tough break, huh?" He leaned against the wall, brushing her shoulder with his. Unless he'd missed his guess, she still wanted him. She'd just been overcome with a bout of conscience. But that wasn't something Brent intended to let get in their way. Not if he could help it.

"Someone might find us."

"They might, but…" He trailed off into a shrug. The implication was clear enough. It was a big party. No one would miss them.

She turned to face him, her eyes wide and soft and hesitant. He intended to erase all her hesitations. "Then we're stuck until morning."

"Afraid so." She closed her eyes as he traced her cheek with his finger, then dipped down to follow the delicate curve of her neck. "Any ideas how we can possibly entertain ourselves all night…?"

A small shiver shook her body, and when she opened her eyes, the longing he saw there cut straight to his gut.

"I shouldn't have started this."

"But you did." With infinite patience, he traced her cheek, delighting when she moaned under his touch. "You started it, and now I want to finish it. So what's it going to be, sweetheart? Naughty? Or nice?"

## CHAPTER THREE

WHAT DID SHE WANT? Brent's question hung in the air, and Annie fought to find a coherent answer.

Earlier, it had all seemed so simple—she wanted Brent. But she'd never expected her desire to be reciprocated. Hell, she'd expected him to balk. She'd flirt and tease and tempt him, but she hadn't actually expected him to say yes so easily. Had she?

But he *had* said yes. In fact, his affirmative response had been quite enthusiastic. Which meant that her foolhardy, wine-induced plan was suddenly a reality. And she had absolutely no idea what to do.

"Annie?" His amused grin made him look even sexier than usual. "I sure hope you answer me tonight, because I really don't want to waste this opportunity."

She stumbled backward, unable to think. His scent did something to her insides. Something wonderful, yes, but it made it hard to keep her thoughts in order. "I should never have—"

"Come on to me so strong you just about melted my insides?" Amusement danced on his moonlit features. "So you said. But you did. And I liked it. And now I want to know what you want to do about it."

He'd moved toward her as he spoke, and now she was backed up against a stack of boxes, unable to escape. What she wanted was to press against him and demand that he kiss her with all the passion she saw reflected in his eyes.

But what she should do...well, that was something entirely different. Before, she'd just wanted Brent. But bumping into Brent's father had reinforced how different their lives were—and that she was playing with fire. Ultimately, she'd be the one who got burned.

She couldn't conjure words, and when his finger curved under her chin, tilting her head back, her silence was assured. A little voice in the back of her mind screamed that she should protest, run, *anything,* to get away.

But she wanted this, Lord help her, she did, and when he lowered his lips to hers, all she could do was moan and open her mouth in silent invitation.

His arms tightened around her waist, pulling her against him into the warm curve of his body. "Are you sure? If you're not, say so now, because, dammit, Annie, I've wanted this for too long. I don't think I can stop if this goes much further."

"Wanted this?" Wanted *her?*

Common sense told her she should stop this. But instead of protests, she heard her own voice, husky and raw, whispering, "I'm sure. Don't stop. Please, don't stop."

He took the invitation to heart, tasting and teasing in a frenzy of passion that left her breathless. Her own enthusiasm matched his, and she wriggled closer as his hands cupped her butt, pressing her tight against him, so tight he would have entered her had it not been for their clothes.

"Please," she whispered.

"Please, what?"

She met his eyes, wanting to lose herself in the pleasure those rich blue irises promised. "Touch me."

He needed no more persuasion, and his hands went to work on her costume, undressing her slowly and sensually. Somehow, he managed to lose his own clothes, as well, and before she knew it, he was right there, hot and ready. And she was so very willing.

"I want you, Annie."

"I know." She could see and feel the hard evidence of his desire. "I want you, too."

Silently, she demanded that he enter her, but instead he stroked her breasts, his mouth warring with hers, his sex teasing and tormenting her.

"This is your show, sweetheart," he whispered, and she realized he was waiting for her. It wasn't enough to say she was sure, she had to show him, too. Brent wasn't about to do anything she didn't want to do.

She broke the contact only long enough to fumble for her purse and pull out a condom. He moaned as she sheathed him, but his moan was even more primitive when she placed his hands on her hips, urging him to lift her up, then bring her down, burying himself in her slick heat.

She gasped, wrapping her arms around his neck and her legs around his body as they moved together. Her back was still against the boxes, and she oddly wondered if they would topple over during their lovemaking.

But soon all silly thoughts left her head, leaving her thinking only of Brent, and the way his body felt against hers. A glorious pressure built inside her, and she cried out, shaking and trembling in his arms as he thrust deeper and harder, finding his own climax before they both sank to the ground.

She cuddled next to him, delighted when he kissed the tip of her nose. In a few moments, he surprised her by pulling a sheet over them. "Linen delivery," he explained. "I'll buy this sheet in the morning."

Spent, they snuggled together, and she tried to stay awake, but the warm, coziness of his arms overwhelmed her and she fell asleep, his gentle kiss on her forehead the last thing she remembered.

LIGHT WAS CREEPING in the tiny window when she awoke in the circle of his arms, and for a moment she just lay there, breathing his musky scent, and wondering if she'd ever again in her life feel so cherished. So loved.

*Loved?*

The veil of sleep vanished, and she was fully awake. What on earth had she done? In her ridiculous fantasy, she'd planned on a seduction where she was in charge. She'd get her wish—Brent in her bed—and she'd get him out of her system.

Except nothing had worked out the way she'd planned. Instead of getting him out of her system, he was more ingrained than ever.

Damned inconvenient, considering she was moving to New York in just a few days—and since nothing long-term could ever develop between a Carrington and a Silver. Heck, he'd practically admitted as much when he'd confessed to noticing her in the past, but never approaching her.

No, the best thing to do was cut her losses.

Carefully, she rolled out from under his arm, then stood up and climbed back into her costume. Brent stirred once, but didn't awaken.

Before she could change her mind, she headed for the door. Without the time lock, the door opened easily, and she paused to look back at him. She wanted to stay, but staying meant complications. And right now she needed to follow the path she'd already set for herself. Say her goodbyes, pack her bags, and move to New York.

And she might as well start right now.

With tears welling in her eyes, she pressed her fingers to her lips, then blew him a kiss.

"Goodbye, Brent," she whispered. "And thank you."

## *CHAPTER FOUR*

BRENT STRETCHED, seeking Annie's warmth even from the depths of his dreams. *Nothing.* His eyes flew open and he bolted upright, a choice curse escaping his lips.

She was gone. The most wonderful night of his life, and the woman he'd shared it with had walked out on him.

Frustrated, he banged the back of his head against the stack of boxes, trying to decide what to do next. Not that there was really any question. For years, he'd wanted a taste of Annie Silver, and now that he'd had one, he didn't intend to give her up. She was sweet and warm and her honest passion had driven him to the brink. He'd never met a woman like her, and he wasn't about to let her walk away without a fight.

Unfortunately, Annie seemed to have a different idea. But Brent hadn't suffered through an M.B.A. program without learning a few things about negotiating. And the first rule was to know your opponent. He knew Annie. He'd watched her for years, wishing he'd been brave enough to assert himself against his father and ask out the smartest, sweetest girl in the school. But he never had, and now he was kicking himself for it.

And the one thing he still didn't know was why she'd come on to him in the first place, or, more important, why she'd walked away.

But he did know someone who might.

"GIVE IT UP, FAITH. I know you know what she's up to." Faith and Annie had been inseparable since elementary school, and even now they were roommates.

Faith held up a finger as she handled the bill for one of the regulars at her little café by the river. As soon as the customer left, she focused on him. "What do you mean 'what she's up to'?" She looked him up and down, clearly taking in his rumpled outfit. "Seems to me you figured that out last night."

If she was trying to fluster him, it wasn't going to work. "I figured out that she wanted a fling. Believe it or not I'm pretty astute at picking up on those subtle little clues."

Faith's mouth twitched, and he knew he'd scored a few points.

"What I hadn't figured on was her bolting. What the hell's up with that?"

"How should I know? Nerves, maybe?"

"She wasn't too nervous to try to seduce me."

"Maybe she thought you didn't want to be seduced." As soon as she spoke, Faith's shoulders slumped, and her eyes darted away. Brent picked up on the signals easily enough—she hadn't meant to reveal that little tidbit.

But why would Annie want to seduce him if she didn't think he'd want her? Or maybe she'd thought she could convince him—he was a guy, after all—but that the most that would happen would be one night of hot and heavy lust. Something simple they could walk away from.

But nothing about last night had been simple. He'd never experienced the kind of closeness he'd felt with Annie, and he was certain she'd felt it, too—and it had scared her enough to send her scurrying away.

The door to the apartment over the café burst open, and Annie bounded in. She stopped cold the second she saw Brent. He clutched the countertop, fighting the urge to go toward her, to hold her.

She swallowed, the flush on her cheeks making her look more adorable as she calmly walked toward them. "Brent. Hi." She licked her lips. "What are you doing here?"

"Looking for you. And trying to figure out why you left."

"I…" Her eyes darted to Faith, but her friend only held up her hands and backed away.

"Don't drag me into this. I already said more than I should have."

Annie's shoulders slumped. "Faith…"

"Don't blame her," Brent said. "I threatened her with bodily harm."

Her expression shifted, and though she tried to hide it, he could see the flash of amusement under her tight features.

"Neither one of you should be talking about me," she said.

Brent moved closer, overcome by the urge to touch her. "Why not, when you're such an enticing subject?" He took her hand, cutting off her answer. "I want you, Annie. I thought I made that perfectly clear last night."

Her lips pressed together before she lifted her eyes to his. "We had our one night." She took a deep breath. "I'd appreciate it if we could chalk it up to hormones and wine and a party atmosphere and just be friends."

"Not gonna happen." He urged her closer, pleased when she didn't fight his gentle tug. "You started this, sweetheart. And I don't think we're anywhere near finished."

Annie's pulse beat an unsteady rhythm as Brent's deep blue eyes bored into her. When she'd come up with her plan to seduce him, she'd never imagined the kind of connection that had sparked between them in the basement.

She'd run because she was scared. And now, because nothing between them could be permanent, she had to keep running.

"It can't work, Brent," she said as soon as he'd steered her into a corner booth.

"What can't?"

"You. Me. There can't be anything permanent here."

"Why not?"

"This isn't *Twenty Questions*."

Leaning across the table, he clasped her hands. "I want to know. Why can't it work?"

She tried to remember all the reasons—it was hard to think with him touching her. "For one, we come from totally different backgrounds."

He made a noise in the back of his throat, and she wondered if that argument had missed its mark.

"My job, for another. I'm moving in January."

That excuse seemed to resonate a little better. "I thought you loved the library."

"I do. Except that my master's is in rare books. Not a whole lot of use in Bishop." She sat up a little taller, still proud of herself for landing her new job. "I'm going to work at the Metropolitan Museum. I'm moving to New York."

His eyes widened, and he grinned, as if she'd just said she wanted to move in with him, rather than that she was moving all the way to Manhattan. Odd.

"So you really did want one wild night. And now you're just going to walk away."

*No!* That might have been her plan, but now so much had changed. Except…she wouldn't give up her dreams, not even for Brent. So in the end, she simply said, "Yes."

"How long before you move?"

"Right after the holidays."

He slid closer, following the curve of the bench seat until his hand rested on her knee, his warmth tantalizing even through the jeans she'd changed into. "Then I suggest we make the most of the time we have." He traced a finger up her thigh, the light touch sending shivers through her body.

"What—?" She broke off, unable to concentrate. "I don't understand."

"You wanted a hot time. So that's what I'm proposing. We'll have a fling hot enough to melt Frosty the Snowman." He caught her eye, his grin full of decadent possibilities. "I'm proposing a full-blown Christmas affair."

A fling? Days and nights in Brent's arms before she left for the harsh streets of Manhattan? Leaving would be harder, the more accustomed she became to being in his arms. But right then, she didn't care about later. She only cared about now. And about Brent.

"All right," she said, flashing him what she hoped was a seductive smile. "Until I leave, I'm all yours."

# CHAPTER FIVE

*ALL YOURS.* Her words echoed as they drove to his apartment. As soon as she'd uttered those two simple words, his entire body had reacted, practically bursting into flames merely from the anticipation of touching her again. He had no idea how this woman could affect him so deeply. He only knew that somehow they had made magic together, and he intended to keep the magic alive.

Pushing open his door, he ushered her in.

"This is nice," she said politely, her gaze skimming over the bare walls and boring furniture.

Brent shrugged. He'd never intended to make the apartment home; he'd simply detoured when his father had insisted he come back home after receiving his M.B.A.

Silently, he took her hand. Their night in the basement had been wild and fast. This time he intended to take it more slowly. With nice little amenities like a mattress. And pillows.

When they reached his bedroom, her eyes danced with mischief. "And this is even nicer."

"Glad you think so. I thought we might be spending some time here."

She glanced at her watch. "Not too much time, unfortunately. I'm working the evening shift at the gift-wrap table."

He slipped his finger into the waistband of her jeans and tugged her closer, delighting when she wrapped her arms around his neck. "Yeah? Well, right now, I'm interested in unwrapping."

"Oh? Maybe you better demonstrate so I know just what you have in mind."

His fingers fumbled at the button of her jeans, then slowly tugged the zipper down as she drew in one short, quick breath. "I think that can be arranged."

As he slipped his hands down inside her jeans and over her hips, he wanted to take it slowly and sensually, but there was no way he could finesse the moment. Not with her sexy little wriggle as she helped him urge the jeans down over her hips and thighs. Then, when she was standing there in only her sweater and panties, well…certainly there was no going slowly then.

And when she peeled the sweater over her head and stood before him in just her underwear, Brent groaned, deep and desperate.

"You're torturing me here, Annie."

"I'm torturing you? I thought you were doing

the unwrapping.'' She stepped forward, her hands going to his zipper. ''Or are you passing off that job?''

No use. He couldn't take it. Her nearness was intoxicating, and he caught her mouth with his, his hands pressing against the small of her back as he pulled her close against him. The heat between them blossomed, and she moaned, grinding against him in a rhythmic motion designed to drive him completely insane.

Somehow he managed to maneuver them to the bed, stripping off his shoes and jeans as they went. At the moment, he wanted nothing more than to sink deep inside her, and the fact that his clothes hadn't dissolved from sheer will frustrated him.

''Please,'' she whispered, her fingers fumbling at the waistband of his boxers. *''Now.''*

The passion in her voice went straight to his heart, even as the blood rushed to other parts of his body. ''Whatever the lady wants,'' he whispered, as his fingers caressed her soft, secret parts.

''The lady wants you,'' she said, her fingernails digging in to his back as she urged him closer. ''She wants you now.''

He'd wanted to take it slowly, but no human male could resist, and Brent was only human. With one quick thrust, he drove into her, losing himself to the exquisite pleasure. She bucked up, meeting him thrust for thrust, their bodies becoming slick with effort, until her climax matched his and he collapsed on top of her, his body limp and spent.

"Mmm." She turned her head, nuzzling his shoulder.

With his thumb and forefinger, he traced a lazy pattern around her nipple. "I'd planned to take it slow. But you're a hard woman to resist."

"Yeah?" She rolled back, her eyes dancing with playfulness. "We still have a little time left. You wanna try again? They say practice makes perfect."

"Sweetheart," he said, rolling her on top of him, "I think you just made me an offer I can't refuse."

An hour later, she dozed beside him, her skin glowing in the afternoon sun that crept through the shades. And as he watched the gentle rise and fall of her chest, Brent knew one thing for certain—no matter what he'd told Annie, he wanted more than a Christmas fling. He always had.

Now he just had to figure out how to convince Annie that he really wanted her by his side. For good.

THEY HELD HANDS during the drive to Carrington's Department Store, the warmth from his fingers spreading through her body all the way down to her toes. Somehow, the moment was even more intimate than the glorious three hours they'd just spent together in Brent's apartment.

"I think this may be the first time I wish I could miss working in Santa's Village."

He turned away from the road long enough to look at her, his cheek dimpling with his smile. "I'm flattered. You've worked there every Christmas since high school." He paused, then looked back at the road. "Why have you?"

Though the question surprised her, his voice held a note of genuine curiosity, and she tried to come up with an answer—something more articulate than *it feels right.* That wasn't a reason for anything. Heck, Brent felt right, but that didn't mean they were going to have a happily-ever-after. Did it?

She shook off the thought, focusing instead on his question. "A lot of reasons, I suppose. But mostly, I love Christmas. The spirit of giving and sharing. The looks on those kids' faces when they sit on Santa's lap. Maybe it sounds corny, but it's heartwarming."

Brent pulled into the employee parking garage, his face passive. "I suppose."

She shifted in her seat to look at him better. "What, Ebenezer? You don't agree?"

She'd expected a smile and a quick denial. Instead, he simply looked sad.

"Let's just say that in my experience, Christmas

has been equated with profit margins. And Christmas Eve was spent waiting for Dad to get home from closing the store and checking the books. I don't think I saw him on the night before Christmas once until I was sixteen and started working at Carrington's. To me, it always seemed as if the customers were racing to see who could buy bigger and better, and my dad was right there, cheering them on. I don't think that's what the spirit of Christmas is all about.''

"No, it's not," she agreed.

"And on Christmas Day my dad never even made an appearance. Just slept until well after lunch, too exhausted to do any sort of family stuff. Not a very Norman Rockwell-esque situation." He shrugged. "Let's just say Christmas isn't my favorite time of the year. Somehow, it all seems like a big con to me."

His words were harsh, but he squeezed her hand, as if trying to assure her that he was fine with the situation. But fine or not, it seemed so sad, and as she followed him into the store, Annie tried to imagine what the holiday season would be like without her family traditions. Pretty miserable, she decided, and she felt sorry for the little boy Brent had been who'd missed out on Santa and cookies and all the stuff she'd grown up with.

Right then, she made up her mind. Before she

went to New York, she'd just have to make sure that Brent got the chance to experience some good, old-fashioned Christmas cheer. And she was just the girl to show him.

# CHAPTER SIX

BRENT FROWNED as he watched Annie working at Santa's Village, looking good enough to eat in her little green elf costume. He shook his head. It was all so commercial, and yet she seemed to be having the time of her life. Her face glowed as she chatted with the children in line to see Santa. And she handled every package she wrapped as though it contained a Fabergé egg, picking out the perfect paper and making sure the package sparkled even though the service was free.

Baffling.

"Excuse me." A gray-haired woman tapped his elbow. "I'm trying to find a gift for my grandson. It's this little electronic gizmo that plays games."

Brent stifled a smile. He might not normally work in toys, but he knew Game Boy when he heard it described. He wanted to tell her that she should get her grandson something cheaper and spend more time with him, but he didn't know this woman and he couldn't presume to lecture her. So in the end, he showed her the display.

Immediately, her face fell. "Oh, dear."

"Problem?"

"I didn't realize they were so expensive."

At least she wasn't reaching into her purse for a credit card with the attitude that debt at Christmas wasn't really debt.

"Thank you anyway, young man."

She was walking away when he noticed her threadbare clothes and her scuffed-up shoes. He had no idea what possessed him, but before he could stop himself, he'd called out to her to wait.

She paused, looking back at him with a curious expression.

"This is completely my fault," he said. "I don't usually manage this department, and I forgot to have the staff put up the sale sign." He held out the box to her. "This one's on sale today only for fifteen dollars."

A huge discount, but the store could afford it. And if his dad disagreed, well, Brent would cover it from his own pocket.

The second he spoke the words, he knew he'd made the right decision. The woman's face lit up like…well, like a Christmas tree.

"I can just about afford that." She took the box that he'd initialed with the new price and clutched it to her chest. "My grandson has to spend Christmas in the hospital. I don't normally approve of these kinds of toys, but he wants one, and I think it will be a nice distraction for him when the family can't be there."

Brent was probably imagining it, but he thought that when she walked away there was a new spring in her step.

"That was an awfully nice thing you just did."

*Annie's voice.* He turned around to see his favorite elf grinning at him from behind a stack of Harry Potter merchandise.

"Could be habit-forming," he said.

She eased over, taking his hand and then urging him toward the employee break room. "Sure could. You just might end up enjoying Christmas after all."

He shrugged. She was teasing, but there was truth to her words. "I've been watching a woman I know. And thinking. She's not too bad a teacher."

"Yeah?" She slipped closer, and his arms automatically closed around her waist. "I can think of a few things you could teach me." She brushed her lips over his. "I've got five minutes left on my break. Maybe a quick lesson is in order?"

Not one to miss an opportunity, Brent leaned over and locked the door. The other employees could wait five minutes for a break.

And once those five minutes were up and he lost Annie to Santa, Brent intended to go have a little talk with his father about what Brent did and didn't want.

For one thing, he didn't want to work in sales. He never had. For another, he wanted Annie, and he intended to get her. His father's approval be damned.

He was twenty-eight years old. It was about time he set the record straight.

BRENT'S FINGERS STROKED her back, leaving a trail of fire that eliminated any lingering chill from the December air. He'd said they were only taking a five-minute break, but Annie wanted so much more than that. Ten minutes, an hour...

*A lifetime.*

She banished the thought. They'd agreed to a fling, and she was content to keep her end of the bargain. Well, maybe not content, but she knew she had no choice. Already, she'd shared more with Brent than she ever thought possible. She should count her blessings. She should rejoice.

Maybe. But the truth was, she only felt sad.

"Penny for your thoughts," he whispered, his breath tickling her ear.

"Nope. I'm not that cheap." She grinned up at him, trying to shake the mood, wanting just to enjoy the moment. "Just hold me, okay?"

He seemed to understand what she needed, and

he pulled her tight, surrounding her with his strong arms as she buried her face against his chest. An innocent touch, but it burned through her just the same.

She clung to him, swaying slightly in his arms, knowing that, for the moment at least, she was secure.

His lips grazed her forehead, moving down to skim over the top of her ear, sending a swarm of shivers racing through her body. Sweet torture, but he kept it up, exploring her ear and her neck with his tongue, his breath hot against her throat.

Her pulse picked up tempo, and she felt her heart beat against his chest. She was barely cognizant of where he ended and she began. "Brent," she murmured.

"I know," he said. And she was certain that he did understand. They'd come together so fast, and yet he already meant so much to her.

"Will I see you after work tonight?"

"Sweetheart, you'd be hard-pressed to keep me away." He stroked her cheek. "What is it about you? So quiet and sweet, and yet you've got my insides all whipped up like a tornado."

"Just my innate charisma, I guess," she said with a grin. She hoped she sounded lighthearted, but the fact was, he was describing the very way she felt about him. And the knowledge that they were so in sync was almost as erotic as his soft touches and caresses.

"That's gotta be it," he said, pulling her close. They held each other, exploring, tasting, and touching, until he pulled away, gently framing her face with his hands. "Five minutes," he said, as she silently cursed whoever invented the very first clock. "Back we go."

She nodded, and he kissed the very tip of her nose.

The moment was so sweet, so tender, and yet she couldn't help the tears that welled in her eyes. In just a few days, she was leaving for New York for a new life. A better life.

But could it really be better if it meant that she'd be alone?

## CHAPTER SEVEN

*BANG, BANG, BANG!*

Brent frowned, confused, until he realized the steady beat was coming from someone knocking at the door. His five minutes of bliss in the break room was over, and now it was time to go back to work.

Looking slightly embarrassed, Annie straightened her costume and her hair and stepped back, then took a seat at the table and started perusing a two-year-old copy of *People* magazine.

Hiding a grin, Brent flipped the lock, and Paul barged in, still in his Santa suit, the green of his face almost matching the tint of Annie's elf costume. Immediately, Annie was up and helping him into a chair.

"What's wrong?"

"Dinner," Paul managed, his voice barely a squeak. "At least, I hope that's all it is. But we've got signs all over the place that say Santa'll be back at eight, but I'm not sure I'm even going to be alive at eight."

He lurched forward then, and rested his head between his knees. "Someone just shoot me now."

Brent caught Annie's eyes, easily reading her expression. She was concerned about Paul, but she was just as concerned about the disappointment of those kids.

Well, what the heck? His moment of Christmas spirit with the old woman and the Game Boy had worked out well. Surely this wouldn't be too bad.

Before he could change his mind, he started peeling off his jacket. "I hope you're not contagious. And I hope that's stuffing in that suit, because otherwise it's just going to fall off me."

Annie's mouth opened, but no sound came out.

Paul's head rose just slightly. "You're going to…"

"Yup. Start stripping. Looks like I'm playing Santa."

Surprisingly, the next three hours passed remarkably fast. So fast, and so enjoyably, in fact, that he barely even noticed when Annie came over and whispered that her shift was over and that she'd see him the next day. Right at the moment, he'd been preoccupied with a precocious seven-year-old determined to explain to him why Blitzen was the best reindeer of the bunch.

Now that the kids were gone and the store was closing, Brent was surprised by how invigorated he felt. All in all, it was a week full of surprises. First Annie, now Christmas.

And there were a few more surprises coming, too. Or there would be if he had his way. For one thing, Brent still needed to talk to his dad.

Then he intended to pop over to the jewelry department to buy the perfect Christmas present for his favorite elf.

"I'M HOPELESS, FAITH," Annie said. "Absolutely hopeless." Which was an understatement. She hadn't stopped thinking about Brent in hours. He'd permeated her brain and was oozing out her pores. The man was in her essence, and she didn't know what to do about it.

Faith leaned back against her sofa cushions and popped the top of her beer. "I'll agree with that. What are you hopeless about today?"

Annie stopped pacing in front of the doorway that led down the stairs to Faith's café just long enough to shoot her friend a dirty look. "What do you think?"

Faith put a finger against her cheek and cocked her head. "Hmm. Let me think. Brent?"

"Very astute."

"So what's the problem? From my perspective, you two are hitting it off just fine. Mission accomplished and all that jazz."

"Except I think I got a little bit more than I bargained for."

Faith took another drink, then spread her arm across the back of the couch. "Oh? Tell."

Annie licked her lips, sure that she was blushing. "I think I'm falling in love with him."

Faith laughed. Not exactly the response Annie had been expecting.

She propped her hands on her hips. "Do I laugh at your love life?"

"I'm sorry," Faith said, clearly trying to hold back another round of chuckles. "It's just that that's so yesterday's news."

Annie frowned. "Excuse me?"

"You know. Old news." Faith waved her hand in the air. "I could tell just from watching you two the other day. This is the real deal."

She wanted to deny it, to say she couldn't possibly be falling in love with Brent Carrington. But as fast as it had happened, as whirlwind as it had been, she knew it was true. Brent matched her and filled her in a way no other person ever had. They may have only spent a short time together, but she knew without a doubt that she wanted to spend the rest of her life with him.

"I guess the bigger question is, what are you going to do about it?"

Sucking in a deep breath, Annie stood up

straighter, hoping good posture would give her the courage she needed. "I only see one option, really. I mean, it's a risk. He might not want me." She licked her lips, not liking that prospect at all.

"So what are you saying?"

"Just that as much as I want to move to New York, I want to make this work. I need to at least try." She ran her fingers through her hair, sure in her heart that Brent was worth the sacrifice, and hoping beyond hope that he loved her, too. "I'm thinking I'll keep my job and stay here in Bishop."

Faith's eyes went wide as she focused on something over Annie's shoulder.

"Are you sure that's what you want to do?" The familiar deep voice drifted over her from behind, and her pulse increased as her body reacted automatically to his nearness.

She spun around, wondering just how much of their conversation he'd heard. "Brent! Um, hi."

"Am I interrupting?"

"No, of course not."

"The door was open. I just walked up."

Annie exhaled in relief. If he'd just arrived, he must not have heard *everything*. It might be the truth, but she wasn't yet willing to share her realization that she was falling in love with this man. Not until she was sure that the feeling was reciprocal.

Brent's earlier words settled in, and Annie faced him square on, her brow furrowed. "What do you mean, am I sure that's what I want to do?"

"Staying here," he said, and her stomach tightened. Had she read him wrong? Was this really just a fling for him, and he wouldn't welcome having her near? "Considering your dream job's in New York, staying here seems silly."

"Silly?" She clenched her fists, hoping against hope that he wasn't about to tell her there was nothing between them.

"Well, sure," he said, taking her hands in his. His dimple flashed, and the band around her heart loosened. "What's the point of you being here if I'm living in Manhattan?"

# CHAPTER EIGHT

ANNIE HELD HER BREATH, wondering if she'd heard him right. "You're moving to New York?"

"That's my plan." Brent shrugged. "I was kind of looking forward to you being there, too. But..." He trailed off, amusement dancing in his eyes.

Annie opened her mouth, but couldn't seem to form words.

From behind her, Annie heard the shuffle of pillows. "I think that's my cue to exit," Faith said, then headed down the stairs.

He held out a hand for her, and she came willingly, knowing that in his arms was exactly where she wanted to be—and exactly where she belonged.

Slowly, as if savoring every tiny touch, he traced his finger down her neck, following the V line of her sweater. The room was toasty warm, but she shivered anyway.

His fingers dipped under the cashmere, then traced the lace of her bra. She moaned, low and in the back of her throat. *More.* She wanted to beg for more, but her voice didn't work, and so she could only hope in silence that he understood her desire.

Of course he did, and she stifled a groan of pure pleasure as his rough fingertips met the soft skin of her breast. He grazed her nipple, teasing with the lightest of touches designed to drive her over the edge. "Oh, Brent," she whispered.

"Mmm?"

She wanted answers—wanted to know why he was moving to New York. But she knew he'd tell her soon enough. And right then, she couldn't think anyway. Couldn't even focus. Heck, she could barely form words, managing only to force out her simple request—"More."

With a low, guttural groan, he dipped his lips to her neck, tasting and teasing as he worked his way lower. "Are you very attached to this sweater?" he whispered.

In answer, she grabbed the hem and pulled it over her head. "You can burn it for all I care."

He laughed. "I don't think that's necessary," he said, then kissed a trail from her neck to her breast, teasing the sensitive skin.

His tongue laved her nipple, her skin puckering in a sweet parody of pain. He was torturing her with his hands, stroking and exploring. And with every little touch, she seemed to melt a little bit more.

He still wore a jacket and T-shirt, and she

reached out, urging the jacket over his arms until it dropped to the floor. She concentrated next on her bra, needing to feel nothing but Brent and air against her skin. Releasing the clasp, she wriggled out of the thing, even while managing to wriggle closer to Brent.

"Take your shirt off," she demanded, wanting to melt under his heat.

He complied, then urged her to the couch. She tugged at his waistband. "You need to lose these."

"A woman who knows what she wants," he said. "I like that."

"Yeah?" She cocked her head. "And what is it you want?"

"I figured that was pretty clear by now. I want you, Annie," he said, his voice low and raw. "I want you now, and I want you in New York."

It took every ounce of strength in Brent's body not to make love to her right there. Etiquette, however, suggested that he wait until they reached his apartment, and so they simply cuddled together, curled up in each other's warmth and enjoying the last few minutes before they braved the cold and let Faith have the apartment to herself.

As he stroked her skin, he knew he'd never be happier than when he was with Annie. She made him feel whole. As if he'd been looking for the other half of himself and had finally found it in her.

With a little sigh, she shifted off his lap, nestling against him on the couch as he tightened his arms around her. After a few minutes, she looked up, her eyes wide and questioning.

"Why?"

"Because I want to be near you. I don't want to lose you, Annie. Not ever. Not if I can help it." He reached into his pocket and pulled out the long velvet box. "Merry Christmas."

Her eyes lit up. "But I haven't gotten you anything."

"You've still got time. According to my dad, there are plenty of shopping days left." He nodded to the box. "Open it."

She did, revealing the delicate chain and the silver heart pendant. "Brent, it's beautiful. Thank you."

"You'll always be in my heart." He grinned, lazily stroking her thigh. "And I hope you'll be in my bed, too."

She laughed. "You won't get any argument from me." She paused then, licking her lips.

His heart tightened. Surely she wasn't having doubts. He'd bet his soul that she felt as he did, but what if he'd been wrong? "But?" he urged, taking the plunge.

"But New York." She sat up, pulling away, but

not letting go of his hands as she faced him. "How can you just pack up and leave?"

"Do you want me there?" He had to hear her say it.

"Of course. But you've got your job here. The family business. Everything."

"You mean more." He sighed, then kissed her palm. "I never wanted to work at Carrington's. But Dad pushed, and I gave in, and I ended up with an M.B.A. I didn't want and didn't need. I had a long talk with him this afternoon. He doesn't completely agree, but he's supporting my decision."

"What *did* you want?"

"Law school. I've been thinking about it for a long time, and I recently applied to four schools. I got into all of them. I'm planning on going to Columbia starting next semester."

"Columbia's in New York."

He pulled a face of mock surprise. "You don't say?"

She laughed, then turned serious. "Is that the school you want to go to?"

He saw the insecurity on her face. "It's exactly where I want to be." Brushing away a loose strand of hair, he met her eyes. "I don't want to rush you. If you're not ready, or if you don't want—"

"No!" Her cheeks flushed a delightful shade of

pink. "I mean, of course I want you, too. Can't you tell?"

"I'd hoped." Oh, how he'd hoped.

She nibbled at her lower lip. "What about your dad? I'm not exactly from the same breeding stock as a Carrington."

He laughed, knowing that despite the sarcastic tone she was truly concerned about his relationship with his dad. "Don't worry. We had a long talk. He knows how I feel, and he understands. And he's pretty impressed with you, what with all your academic achievements and now this new job." He shrugged. "My dad's a tough nut, but eventually he cracks."

She snuggled against him. "Good."

He stroked her hair. "I love you, Annie. It hit me fast and hard, but I can't deny the truth. And the truth is, I love you."

"I love you, too," she said, as the weight of the world lifted from her heart. "I think I always have, and I know I always will."

Snuggling back into his embrace, she let out a contented sigh. "Who would've believed it?" she asked.

"What's that?"

"That all my Christmas wishes would come true. And it's not even Christmas yet."

Closing his eyes, Brent hugged her tighter, this woman who, for the first time he could remember, had brought pure joy to him for the holidays…and beyond.